MISSION: IMPOSSIBLE

THE PRICELESS PARTICLE

Authorized Edition

By TALMAGE POWELL

Cover by MICHAEL LOWENBEIN

A WHITMAN BOOK

Western Publishing Company, Inc., Racine, Wisconsin

WHITMAN is a registered trademark of
Western Publishing Company, Inc.

CONTENTS

1   Icing on the IMF Cake   9

2   Enter Miriam Belorra   21

3   A Specialist   40

4   The Favorite Visitor   52

5   At the Diggings   66

6   Arrival in Masarium   82

7   A Capsule   93

8   Miriam and Lara   105

9   The Scene   117

10   Two Escapes   132

11   Man in the Middle   150

12   Reunion   168

13   Confidential Conversation   182

14   "Just Grab and Hang On!"   197

1. ICING ON THE IMF CAKE

ON THAT SUNNY Italian morning, Jim Phelps might have been just another American tourist taking his first gondola ride on the canals of picturesque Venice.

The hotel manager, like everyone else at the luxurious hostelry, had instantly pegged Jim as one of those successful American executives who likes to break away from a desk and get out where the action is. The manager mentioned to the majordomo that the new American would probably be equally effective running a board of directors meeting or out personally taking charge of a critical problem in an oil field.

The manager should know. For thirty years he had done his share in making a Venetian visit a treasured lifetime memory for untold thousands of tourists. He had seen and dealt with every type. He had sound reasons for believing that he could, at first glance, spot a false front even without putting on his delicate pince-nez glasses.

Jim certainly looked the part. His thick hair had a premature-gray sheen that contrasted sharply with his rangy physique and rugged, youthfully vigorous face. His neat gray business suit, traditional in cut, was a hint of Madison Avenue. But the keen-eyed, observant stranger could just as easily have imagined him in safari garb, had he chosen to vacation in another part of the world.

Strictly speaking, Jim's executive look had a solid foundation. But the executive post he filled was the only one of its kind on earth. The outfit he headed wasn't listed in Dun and Bradstreet, and it had no stock for sale on the New York and London exchanges.

His stock-in-trade would have retired most corporation presidents with nervous breakdowns. He was the key man in a group that had no official existence. Those who knew him socially had never suspected his real position. Indeed, there were top people in the American government itself who had never heard of IMF—the Impossible Missions Force—the specialist on call for the job that was too tough for any other agency.

This beautiful morning the traffic on the Grand Canal was heavy, as usual. Small barges and freight gondolas, heaped with fresh vegetables for the markets of Venice, threaded among gondolas carrying tourists of every nationality and color. The very air was warmed by gaiety, good humor, goodwill. From a gondola just ahead of Jim's, a gondolier sang an old Venetian folk song in a rich tenor that would have brought bravos at the Met.

The city of canals was one vast architectural and art treasure dating from the Renaissance. There was just too much for a single pair of eyes to take in, and Jim's gondolier pointed out sights of special interest as he punted their craft along.

"We are now passing the Ca'd'Oro, most sumptuous of fifteenth-century palaces. . . . And this is the masterpiece of design by Longhena, the Palazzo Pesara. It is now another of our many art museums. . . . And there, Senhor!—the finest example of Gothic architecture in the world, the Ca' Foscari. . . ."

Jim wished that he had a month—a year—in which to feast his mind and emotions on the splendid human heritage that was Venice. But he knew that this was not to be. An urgent coded message had directed him to this particular gondola, which even now was putting in at the landing stage in front of the deluxe Danieli Royal Excelsior hotel.

Even though he had checked in but a few hours ago, Jim was under the spell of the hotel. The atmosphere was elegant but relaxing. The food and service were among the world's best. The lounges were pleasant, and the view from the terrace was unlike anything else on earth, encompassing the sweep of fifteenth-century buildings built on the canals.

Riding midway between the up-curving prow and

the gondolier's perch in the stern, Jim rose as the gondola drifted close to the landing stage.

"I wish," he said casually, "that I had a peck of Sundays to spend in Venice."

The gondolier was a short, swarthy man with, strangely, eyes as blue as the Italian sky. His eyes flashed, then veiled as he stepped toward Jim.

"A peck? Of Sundays?" The gondolier smiled. "A quaint expression. I've never heard it before."

Jim said nothing as he waited for the countersign. The gondolier busied himself with the snarl that had somehow gotten in his landing lines. In a moment the gondola that was almost brushing their port gunwales was beyond earshot.

The gondolier raised his face toward Jim's. The balmy breeze fluttered the ribbon streamer on the back of the gondolier's broad-brimmed hat. "You desire a *bushel* of time, Senhor?"

"You read my thought." Jim stretched out his hand, and the gondolier leaned forward to accept the coin.

"*Grazie.*" The amount of the tip might have brought a touch of wry amusement to the gondolier's smile. The coin was only a nickel, American currency. But it had a row of almost invisible stars stamped into Jefferson's collar. The sight of it removed the final flicker of the question that had lurked in the gondolier's eyes.

Jim had stepped onto the landing.

"Senhor!"

Jim stopped and turned.

"You forgot your camera, Senhor."

Phelps returned the few steps to the edge of the

landing. The gondolier tipped his craft slightly as he leaned to hand Jim the rather heavy leather case.

Jim shook out the strap and draped it about his neck. "Thanks a million. I'd hate myself if I got back to Detroit without some color slides!"

As he did a casual broken-field through the crowded hotel lobby, Jim had the passing wish that he had the film from that other camera. The one he had set out with and snapped scenery now and then during his brief trip. The one that was still in the gondola, now that the gondolier had made the switch. He really would have liked some color slides to commemorate his quick sojourn in Venice.

He rode the elevator to the deeply carpeted upper hallway. All thoughts of himself, his own wishes, were wiped from his mind as he hurried to his room and bolted the door behind him.

He moved about quickly, checking the room for electronic bugging devices. Lifted a portrait away from the wall. Ran sensitive fingers underneath the provincial writing desk. Swished back the draperies of the tall windows that opened on the small private balcony. Checked the drapery pull cords and overhead track for possible connections. Moved to the Louis XVI bed and used his fingers to explore the head, foot, sides.

Jim eased to a sitting position on the edge of the bed and flipped the latch of the leather case. It was one of the larger kind, designed to hold a camera plus the gadgets many amateurs like to load up with.

Inside the case was a transistorized tape recorder

and, tucked behind it, a stiff manila envelope.

Jim lifted out the recorder, set it on his knees, and punched the switch. While the first few seconds of silent tape passed from spool to slowly turning spool, Jim peeled the flap from the manila envelope and slid from it a thin sheaf of glossy photographs.

Before he had a chance to study the pictures, the tape recorder began to speak.

"Good morning, Mr. Phelps," the quiet, cultured voice intoned. "A desperate situation has come to our attention. Any delay in attending to it will be disastrous. . . .

"The work of Dr. Hasman Belorra has, so far, escaped wide public attention. Shy and bookish, he has buried himself for years in his laboratory. We may assume that much of the time he was little aware of what was going on in the world outside. He was wealthy, free to do the work that obsessed him—biochemical research.

"However, as a citizen of the poverty-stricken principality of Masacar in the Middle East, Dr. Belorra lived in that half of the world that goes to bed hungry each and every night. He witnessed the misery firsthand—adults with eyes dulled and glazed with starvation, the spindly children too weak from hunger to raise another cry for food.

"In the faces of his own people, Dr. Hasman Belorra saw the starving millions throughout the underdeveloped nations of the earth. He decided to do something about the situation. Giving away his personal fortune, large as it was, wouldn't amount to a crumb. Instead, he made up his mind to devote his fortune—and himself—to attacking the problem at its root.

"Dr. Belorra's basic idea wasn't new. Protein is essential to a proper, healthful diet. Why not mass-produce it? Invent a process so that factories could turn it out by the carload? The same thing has been done with countless other items we use. Many of our miraculous drugs started with somebody building a molecule in a test tube. We don't have to grow cotton any longer to get material for clothing. The rubber in our automobile tires now comes from a factory process instead of a rubber tree.

"Dr. Belorra succeeded where others have failed." The even inflection of the voice gave no hint of the earth-shaking announcement he was making. "He has produced a man-made protein molecule in his laboratory. Further, he worked out the first steps for cheap mass production of his priceless particle.

"No doubt this great, but as yet unhonored, scientist and humanitarian believed the time was near when factories would be pouring out tons of foodstuff for a hungry world.

"But even as Dr. Belorra worked and dreamed, evil forces were at work. Civil disorders were nothing new to Masacar. One government after another came and went, unable to solve the problems of the suffering country. The last government seemed to be making some headway, with help from the West.

"But a certain power-hungry man was plotting. His schemes were encouraged by the Eastern bloc of nations. He is Janar Aqaban, military minister in the previous cabinet. And of course his seizure of total power made world headlines for a while.

"Aqaban poses as a great friend of the people. But he cares nothing for them. Recent history echoes the boot-stamp of men like Aqaban in small, helpless nations all over the world.

"He promises free elections and land reforms, but actually he is dealing secretly with the totalitarian bloc. The bargain is as old as the face of treachery itself. The enemies of the free world swallow up another struggling nation. In exchange, Aqaban will be promised security in his position of a puppet dictator lording it over his own people.

"When Dr. Belorra realized what was really happening in his country, he tried to flee with Miriam, his daughter. Unfortunately, Dr. Belorra was a lot smarter inside his laboratory than outside. He was captured and imprisoned by Aqaban. The details of his work were wrung out of him, you can be sure.

"We have learned of Dr. Belorra's plight from his daughter, who escaped from Masacar and made her way to Rome.

"We have also learned that a Captain Stefan Zovoloff is now being briefed somewhere in Asia to go to Masacar. Clearly, his mission has but one purpose. He will make a deal with Aqaban for the Belorra formula.

"If the totalitarian powers monopolize this fresh new hope of the world feeding itself, I need hardly mention the consequences! As the world population explodes, the poorer nations would one day face a life-

or-chains decision. Freedom's enemies would give them a choice of starvation or surrender.

"We must break this threat before it becomes a fact. We must give the backward peoples a choice other than starvation or totalitarianism. We must give them a chance to develop their own nations—including food factories—as free men.

"Dr. Belorra intended his discovery for all the world, in the spirit of Pasteur and Salk. He didn't design it as a political tool.

"Your mission, should you decide to accept it, is to beat Zovoloff and Aqaban to the punch. Bring Dr. Hasman Belorra and his formula safely out of Masacar.

"As always, should you or any of the IMF force be caught or killed, the Secretary will disavow any knowledge of your actions.

"You may accept this assignment simply by appearing on the balcony outside your window in the next five minutes. This recording will self-destruct in ten seconds."

Phelps gave his head a slight shake. This was just about the icing on previous IMF cakes.

He carried the recorder to the writing desk where he set it down. He turned, and as he recrossed to the bed and picked up the glossy pictures the tape began to disappear in a soft hiss of smoke.

He looked at the pictures with the eyes of a man who could imprint every detail so firmly in his mind that the slightest shift would not escape him.

He looked at the photograph of Dr. Belorra first. He was somewhat surprised. He had expected to see a bespectacled little man with the frugal habits of a mouse. Instead, Belorra was a very youthful middle-age, dark, good-looking. He somehow made Jim think of a husky, trim, Greek athlete.

Aqaban's was not exactly the face of a stranger. As a matter of routine, Jim had studied newspaper and television pictures when Aqaban had strutted to power. The upstart dictator had tried to play down his egotistical, imperious appearance before the cameras. But the cameras had caught it, at least in the case of the one that had taken the picture now in Jim's hands. The lean chin had a cold, haughty cast about the edges. The brows arched ever so slightly over eyes in large sockets, as if Aqaban had a sneering question for the rest of the world.

His own conceit, Jim mused, *might be the weapon against this fellow.*

Captain Stefan Zovoloff was a bird of an entirely different feature. Nothing of foolish, unfounded conceit in these chiseled Nordic features. Just a hard, cold self-assurance that comes when a man knows the fullness of his own powers. Just that *belief* in success. Jim had a hunch the belief was well-founded. Zovoloff had the look of a man who had never known failure.

The final picture brought a flick of appreciation to Jim's eyes. Miriam Belorra was the perfect mixture of northern and southern Europe. She had dark blond hair, no doubt from her mother's side of the family. Her cheekbones were rather high. She had wide-set, intelligent eyes that reflected both kindness and determination, and a mouth that would be quick to smile under pleasant circumstances.

Jim dropped the pictures for the moment on the bed and strolled onto the small window balcony.

The gondola he had ridden was still down there. To all appearances, the gondolier was lazily dozing after his tour with the vacationing American.

When Jim appeared three stories above the canal, the gondolier stretched, yawned, straightened up. He gave a nod in the direction of the balcony. Then he punted slowly away on the watery thoroughfare.

Back in his room, Jim crossed to the two-suiter that rested on a stand near the chest of drawers. He took his key case from his trousers pocket, opened it, and flipped out what looked like an ordinary key. He pressed its edges between his fingers. The key popped into two halves. It was a shell, a scabbard for the thin strip of case-hardened steel that was inside.

He lifted the suitcase lid, revealing a neatly packed brown suit and half a dozen neckties. He inserted the tiny steel tool beneath the latch. His fingers moved carefully. The slightest tampering with the suitcase would cause its contents to go up in a flash.

A click sounded within, and the false bottom was released. Jim rumpled the suit and ties slightly as he swung the bottom on its hidden hinges. He lifted out a flat, black file case, crossed the room, and sat down.

Opening the file case, he began sliding out the dossiers of IMF agents.

Each picture he looked at reminded him of assignments here and there all over the world. Good moments—and some very hairy ones.

He studied a picture, shook his head, then chose the next. When he had finished picking through the file, he had removed four pictures. He propped the case beside the chair and looked at the pictures.

"Hi, Cinnamon," he said to the picture on top. The girl in it was fair-haired and lovely. But Jim was more interested at the moment in the brains and cool courage behind that attractive exterior.

The next picture was that of a man with dark hair inclined to crinkle, an aquiline nose, and a full strong chin. His name was Rollin Hand. He hadn't quite hidden the daredevil glint in his eyes, nor the theatrical look.

Jim slid the next picture to the top. It was of Barney Collier. The face of the young Negro was firm, strong. The eyes had that kind of serious dedication that Jim more than admired. He liked to have it working with him when the going promised to be really rough. Barney's headful of mathematical formulae was also very handy to have around.

The final picture made Jim think of an immovable object in the forward wall of a football team, or massive barbells being lifted from the floor. But for all his strength, the dark-haired ruggedness of Willy Armitage reflected a certain gentleness.

Jim returned the dossiers to the black file. The team was chosen, complete. Cinnamon Carter. Rollin Hand. Barney Collier. Willy Armitage. And, of course, Jim Phelps.

I wonder, Jim reflected, *how many we have stacked against us?*

ENTER
2. MIRIAM BELORRA

A FEW HOURS LATER Phelps was at a small villa on the outskirts of Rome. Officially, the Italian government was following a hands-off policy in the internal affairs of Masacar. But a high-ranking minister had offered the house to Miriam Belorra as a private guest.

From the front porta, Jim could look across a small piazza, a splashing fountain, lawns hemmed with neat box hedges, and arbors of flowers. He didn't see the ever-present *poliziotto*, but he knew they were out there. The government had no intention of permitting Aqaban's agents to run Miriam Belorra to earth and violate Italian law.

Beyond the piazza and landscaped grounds, a

narrow cobblestone road wound through a stand of
tall poplar trees and across lazy meadows. Past fields
marked by ivy-grown fences of stone, the road disappeared at last over a low hill. Farther on, Jim knew, it
linked to the modern highway sweeping north from
Rome.

Through a break in the trees, Jim glimpsed a small
car stirring a fantail of dust as it raced over the bumpy
road. The car slowed and turned off on the driveway
that twined to the villa.

Jim turned from the outside view and moved across
the foyer into the coolness of a spacious room with a
towering, beamed ceiling. There were tapestries on
the walls, a bronze shield over the rustic fireplace.
The furnishings were similar to those in a hunting
lodge—massive couches and chairs, and huge, shaggy
rugs.

"Our friends are in sight," he said. He glanced at his
wristwatch. "And arriving right on time."

Miriam Belorra looked at Jim from the depths of a
leather chair. Her eyes still had a slightly glazed look.
Jim wasn't surprised. He knew how hard his unexpected appearance must have hit her. She'd known
nothing but defeat and despair for quite a while. Then
he, a capable-looking stranger, had appeared to offer
the first glimmer of hope for bringing her father out
of Masacar to safety.

Jim saw the whiteness in her knuckles as she
gripped the arms of the heavy chair. He felt the pressure of her gaze as she scrutinized him for the
dozenth time.

Her first reaction had been cautious. This hadn't surprised him, either. She'd been through too much to trust anyone blindly. And even though his words and credentials were convincingly genuine, did she dare to take the risk he spoke of? Her father was in a trap that looked unbreakable, but at least he was alive. Should she make a move that might risk what little was left?

Jim hadn't pressed the point. She knew the score, the meaning of her father's work to the world of the future. The decision had to be hers.

She breathed in slowly as a shaft of sinking sunlight caught in her dark blond hair.

"I love my father dearly, Mr. Phelps. I have to put his interests above anything else."

Jim took a short breath of disappointment. He'd counted on her. She'd taken plenty on the chin, but after talking with her, he'd believed that she was game for more.

"The decision is not really mine, Mr. Phelps," she was saying. "It has to be my father's."

"Too bad he isn't here to tell us," Jim said.

She gave him a little quirk of a smile. "He's not entirely absent. Some part of him is here." She closed her eyes for a moment. Jim watched the shifting expressions of her face as her mind dwelt on precious memories. "I know what my father would want me to say to you, Mr. Phelps."

"And what is that?"

She looked at him thoughtfully. "How do you Americans put it?" The faintest hint of a smile tugged her mouth. "Let's get the troops out of the hot sun and put this show on the road!"

Jim laughed. "No one could have put it better. Thanks, Miss Belorra."

"Thanks? No, the thanks should be the other way around." Now that she had made up her mind, a weight seemed to have lifted. Natural vitality and spunkiness glinted in her eyes.

She sprang from her chair. "Now, Mr. Phelps . . . what do we do first? How long will it be before I can see Papa? What is your plan? When can I. . . ."

"Easy there!" Jim smiled as he flung up a restraining hand. "Let's shift to a lower gear. We've many details to think about, you know."

He broke off as the Indian elephant bells tinkled outside the front porta. Turning from Miriam, he hurried across the room and through the foyer.

The porta framed the heavy figure of a *poliziotto*. "Sorry to trouble you, Senhor Phelps. It is a matter of security regulations."

The man moved aside a few inches and hooked a thumb over his shoulder. "I'm sure they are your people, but I must have your confirmation."

Jim looked past the plainclothesman. Beyond the piazza, the car, a Porsche, had stopped in the driveway. Cinnamon, Barney, Willy, and Rollin had gotten out. They stood quietly beside the car under the watchful eyes of two more Italian agents who had seemed to materialize from nowhere.

Jim nodded. "They are the four I expected."

"*Buono*. Then everything is in order." The man

turned and made a small signal with his hand. The men watching the car nodded, then gestured permission for the IMF team to proceed.

The four hurried across the piazza, up the shallow stone steps, and came upon Jim with a rush.

Their voices bubbled.

"Hi, Jim. . . ."

". . . looking great. . . ."

". . . blasted cablegram caught me about to sneak a vacation. . . ."

"What's the current hangup?"

Jim looked at each face fondly while the bantering went on. Cinnamon's contralto, Barney's professorial tone, Willy's blunt baritone, and Rollin's theatrical delivery made a pleasant blend in Jim's ears.

"Come on," he said. "I want you to meet the ex-officio member we're including on the team this time."

Linking his arm with Cinnamon's, Jim led the way across the foyer and into the sunken living room.

Miriam Belorra was standing expectantly in the middle of the room. The IMF team crowded about and Jim introduced them one by one.

After she'd shaken hands with each, Miriam Belorra said, "Something to drink while we talk? I have tea. American style, no less—with plenty of ice."

The afternoon was hot, and the team murmured a grateful thanks. As Miriam crossed to a hand-carved buffet and busied herself with a silver tea service, the IMF people settled on couches, chairs, and hassocks that faced each other.

Miriam was among them in an instant with a tray

bearing tall glasses, a bowl of ice, and a pitcher of tea. While she served, Jim eased back in his chair and got right down to business.

"The problem may be stated in the proverbial nutshell. It's our job to bring Miriam's father, Dr. Hasman Belorra, safely out of Masacar."

The others exchanged quick glances. Willy whistled softly between his teeth. Cinnamon's hand froze with her glass halfway to her mouth. Barney rolled his eyes heavenward.

Rollin gave Jim a lofty Shakespearean look. "Do my ears deceive me?"

"Not a bit." Jim grinned.

"Nutshell he calls it," Willy growled.

"Iron nutshell—since Janar Aqaban took over the country and sealed it tighter than a tin of sardines," Barney said.

"That's right," Rollin agreed. "We'll have to dream up a real nutcracker for this one!"

"Sounds like two problems to me," Cinnamon said. "First, we have to get in—then we have to get out."

"And between lies the middle problem," Rollin said, "the problem of staking out a claim on Dr. Hasman Belorra."

Willy shook his head. "And he's not baggage we can tuck in a pocket, like plans for an atomic installation." He glanced at Miriam. "Meaning no disrespect to your father, ma'am."

"Maybe," Barney said half-jokingly, "our old master of disguises, the one and only Rollin Hand, can dress you up to look like Aqaban, Willy. Then you can deport us freedom-loving foreigners as undesirable aliens."

Willy snorted, then fixed the young Negro with a glower. "That's supposed to be funny? You may dig tensor calculus—but a Flip Wilson you're not!"

Rollin's eyes were hard on Jim's face. "Haven't I read somewhere that Dr. Hasman Belorra is a biochemist?"

Jim nodded. "He's never had much publicity, like many scientists who've toiled for years before the completion of work that burst them suddenly into the public eye. But I imagine that Barney has run across the nature of his work in scientific journals."

Barney squeezed juice from a wedge of lemon into his icy glass. "He's experimented for years with protein molecules, trying to find a way to. . . ." His mouth suddenly hung open, as if he'd received a hard, invisible punch in the stomach. "Jim . . . you mentioned the completion of work. Are you saying that Dr. Belorra succeeded? He's actually put a protein molecule together?"

"Actually." Jim smiled.

Rollin gasped. In the act of stirring his tea, he agitated the liquid over the side of the glass.

Willy glanced from Barney to Rollin to Jim. "The whiz kids seem to dig, but my hep isn't so cool."

"Dr. Hasman Belorra has taken the first step," Jim explained for Willy's benefit. "Factories of the future may use methods based on the Belorra process to turn out food—in unlimited quantities. It won't be a whole diet, but it'll give the world the basic stuff for straight bones and healthy brains."

"Wow!" Willy said. "You mean the way factories nowadays take common stuff and turn it into something it wasn't? Coal tar into medicine, for example?"

"Something like that," Jim agreed.

"And this hope for the future, for children yet unborn, is in Janar Aqaban's hands," Cinnamon said.

"Aqaban hit the jackpot," Rollin conceded, "like the well-digger who struck oil."

"Seems we're a little late," Willy said. "Aqaban's already got the Belorra secret."

"Be content to let us admire your muscles." Rollin sighed. "Food becomes a weapon only if one side can supply it."

The furrow left Willy's brow. "Sure—I'm with it now! If we can offer people a choice, the other side is neutralized."

"Attaboy, Willy!" Rollin applauded.

Jim looked at Miriam Belorra, who had eased to a hassock at the edge of the group.

"Would you move over beside Miss Carter, please? I want Rollin to study the two of you closely together."

Miriam got up and took the few steps to the couch on which Cinnamon sat. Miriam eased down beside her.

Jim gave Rollin a few moments to study the girls. "Well?"

"No problem," Rollin said. "Fact, I should feel miffed at you for thinking there might be. The two are alike in general size and coloration. With a few flicks of my fingers I can transform our own Cinnamon into Miriam Belorra, if that's what you're thinking. Even her own father will be dashed when he discovers the difference."

"That's what I was thinking," Jim said. "Do you mind temporary loss of your identity, Miss Belorra?"

"I don't mind anything that will help my father, Mr. Phelps. You give the orders. I am—how do Americans say?—in a very bad frying pan. I'm not afraid of the fire."

"Good." Jim nodded. "You'll have to go back to Masacar with Miss Carter. You'll have to be on hand to coach her about details of your childhood, to keep her from taking a wrong turn in the mere act of walking along the streets. Without your help and guidance, Cinnamon's masquerade as Miriam Belorra might serve only to land her in hot water."

Miriam frowned. "How can this be? Two Miriam Belorras in Masacar at the same time?"

"You leave that to Rollin," Jim said confidently.

Rollin helped himself to a little more of the excellent tea. He tilted his head as he studied the girl. "Let's see. Yes, that should do it . . . I'll make you a few shades darker, change the contour of your very nice face, blacken the hair, alter the color of the eyes. You'll be—a poor girl from Sicily. Or North Africa? Miriam Belorra—meaning Cinnamon—has acquired you as a personal maid while she was in Rome."

Miriam accepted the suggestion eagerly. "Then I will always be at Miss Carter's side to keep her from error while she poses as me!"

"That's the general idea," Jim said. "But it'll be a little trickier than that. You can't be at Cinnamon's elbow every second. You'll have to anticipate situations, play it by ear. And. . . ." He hesitated. "If anything should go wrong, you'll be the only contact between us and Cinnamon."

Miriam looked at Cinnamon gravely. "You can depend on me."

Jim liked the quiet tone in which she said the words. "Let's have a look at the map."

From the inner pocket of his jacket, he removed a neatly folded map. The paper crackled as he got up and spread it on a heavy teakwood table.

The IMF team and Miriam Belorra crowded close.

"Here is Masacar," Jim said. "Its northern boundary is the Mediterranean Sea."

"Quite a swim, even for me," Willy said with a grin.

Jim's fingers traced lines on the map. "Eastern and western Masacar is bounded by small neutral nations. They are too weak to jeopardize themselves. They can't risk an international incident by helping us cross either border."

"Which leaves the south," Rollin said.

"Empty desert," Barney murmured. "A wasteland of burning sand that would fry a camel."

"But the only door for which we have a key," Jim said.

Rollin's hand made a sweep over the area of southern Masacar. "It would take days, even with a Land Rover and all the equipment we'd need for a desert crossing."

"Who said anything about land?" Jim inquired.

"Uh-oh," Willy grumbled. "I get it!" He gingerly patted his iron-hard stomach. "I don't like to travel by parachute. I always get queezy, hanging there and swooshing back and forth like that."

"But just think how good it feels when your feet are back on the ground, Willy," Barney reminded him. "Assuming, of course, that the parachute opens."

Willy speared his brown-skinned friend with a baleful glance. "Why don't you stick with your mathematical curlicues and quit trying to bug me? I'll get airsick any time I'm good and ready!"

Jim's pointing fingers inched from south to north on the map. "Here the desert begins to give way to scrubby farmland. Then a little further north, the strip that yields most of Masacar's scanty food supply —olive and date groves, sheep pastures, grain fields. The capital city, Masarium, is farther north toward the sea, point zero. We four men will go in by night. We'll make a delayed drop, from high altitude so the passage of the aircraft won't attract undue attention. This is the drop point"—his finger stabbed—"just south of the capital. We bury the chutes and take a stroll into the city."

"How about Miriam and me?" Cinnamon asked. "If you fellows have the sky-diving fun, do we just float in on cloud nine?"

"We'll get to that in a moment—and your mode of entry should give you something besides Willy's airsickness to think about," Jim said.

He turned the map over. A detailed drawing of

Masarium, the capital city, was on the reverse.

The city sprawled with indefinite boundaries. Its streets looked like narrow, unplanned squiggles—except for the large square area where the presidential palace stood.

"Masarium was already a stopover and watering place for caravans when Alexander the Great marched East," Jim explained. "The Romans governed the region for a couple of hundred years. They built a procurator's residence on the site now occupied by the presidential palace. The Roman government house was complete with aqueducts bringing in water for the heated baths that no self-respecting Roman ruler could do without.

"After the Romans," Jim continued, "came Syrians, Moslems, Crusaders. Everybody and his brother occupied or destroyed Masarium at one time or another. But the people always came back to rebuild their city on the ruins. Like many cities in that part of the world, present-day Masarium is several levels higher than the original town."

"Little wonder it's an archaeological treasure," Rollin said. He was referring to the explorations of the lower levels that had been started by the previous government.

"The digging is one activity that Aqaban hasn't stopped," Jim said. "He confiscates the priceless ancient artifacts as they're turned up. But"—Jim's eyes glinted—"he might also have given us a certain advantage without knowing it."

A small sob came suddenly from Miriam Belorra.

The map of familiar streets and landmarks had roused too many memories.

Cinnamon slipped her arm about Miriam's shoulder.

"All I can see," Miriam said in a choked voice, "are the walls of the presidential palace. My father—if he still lives—hidden somewhere behind those walls. Even if you pull one miracle after another—get into Masacar, into Masarium . . . into the walled palace grounds themselves—Aqaban's men will be swarming everywhere."

The weight of the past weeks of flight and despair seemed to engulf Miriam. "It is too much, now that we actually come to think of it all."

It was bigger than she knew. But this was no time to speak of the agent, Stefan Zovoloff, flying in from Asia. Jim decided he could brief the others on Zovoloff later. Things were coming too fast at the troubled girl already. Cinnamon could tell her about Zovoloff when the right time came.

"If it wasn't impossible," Rollin said gently, bracing the girl with a smile, "we wouldn't trouble ourselves to be here."

"We're not licked—until we quit," Jim added. "If we start, we won't turn back. Shall we start, Miriam?"

She closed her eyes. Her face was white. Jim knew she was filled with memories. The good days, a pleasant home, a loving father who would forget sometimes to come from his laboratory at mealtime. She was thinking of the sudden ending of it, the nightmarish flight. She was hearing her father's stern order for her to make for the border while he led Aqaban's thugs a chase in the south. Again, in the dark halls of her mind, she was begging her father to let her stay with him, remembering his refusal, his assurance that he would make it and meet her in Cairo.

He hadn't, of course. Instead, in Cairo she had spotted a pair of Aqaban's men watching her apartment, making sure it was really she before they closed in. She'd known then that the worst had happened. She'd guessed the terrible things that had gone on behind the palace walls as Aqaban wrested the formula from her father.

She'd used the last of her money to buy a plane ticket for Rome. She had friends in Rome, and their interest and generosity had brought her to this moment.

Jim watched her shoulders brace. She opened her eyes, and as he looked into them Jim knew she had settled the issue inside of herself once and for all.

"I don't like the idea of quitting, Jim. It—how say you—bugs me!"

Cinnamon gave her shoulders a squeeze. "You are— how we say—strictly with it!" Cinnamon glanced at Jim. "But our cloud-floaters still haven't suggested a way for a couple of girls to get into Masarium."

"You'll drive in," Jim said.

"Just like that?"

"Why not?" Jim grinned. "The minute you, as Miriam Belorra, and Miriam, as a personal maid you acquired in Rome, hit the first border checkpoint—"

"We'll be huffed off straight to Aqaban," Cinnamon broke in.

"Sounds like a cool idea," Barney said.

"Oh, sure." Cinnamon gave an airy wave of her hand. "If you don't mind sending a helpless (girl) straight into. . . ."

"Helpless!" Rollin exploded.

The men joined his burst of laughter. Cinnamon treated them to a glare, then lifted her brows at Miriam Belorra. "With such friends, a (girl) needs enemies such as Aqaban?"

"Color Aqaban's future dark," Jim suggested, sobering. "Now for the final, tactical details. . . ."

The freight compartment of the small, swift cargo airplane was dimly lighted and gripped by the numbing coldness of high altitude.

In jump gear, Phelps crouched on the narrow metal slat that served as a seat against the side of the fuselage. Strung closely beside him were Barney, Willy, and Rollin. Almost touching Willy's toes was the bulky equipment package with its own parachute. Willy had to see that it, as well as himself, cleared the aircraft.

In the faint light Jim's face was a pale triangle below his padded leather helmet. He looked at his watch.

Any second now. . . .

He lifted his eyes to the aluminum bulkhead that closed off the pilot's cabin. As if his thought had been a clicking switch, a small green light at the top of the bulkhead suddenly winked on.

"Ready!" Jim's voice was tight. "The pilot is about to make the final radar reckoning to pinpoint the drop."

He was rising as he spoke, slipping a few feet forward in a crouch. He slid open the side hatch. A small hurricane blasted into the cabin. The whine of the jets was ear-splitting. It ruled out further talk.

Jim gripped the sides of the open hatch, his body coiled to spring. He felt Barney brush against his backpack as the others crowded forward.

A dryness seeped through his mouth. He felt his heartbeat as it raced a little faster. He looked at the pale reflections of the moonlight on the white, puffy softness of cumulus clouds drifting five thousand feet below. The cover was better than he'd expected.

He turned his head and watched the small bulkhead light. It wasn't the sort of mass jump he favored, with everyone going out almost on the instant. But they must take no chances of wide separation on the ground.

The plane suddenly seemed a leaden weight hanging on nothing in the sky as the pilot cut back power. The small, green light winked off.

Jim gasped in a breath and willed his muscles to action. He felt the rush of air that meant he was in free fall. He spread his arms and maneuvered his body to keep himself from tumbling.

The clouds below seemed to be drifting up toward him. His blood sang with the exhilaration of a long sky dive. He knew he was approaching terminal velocity, the fastest rate at which an object can fall through a sea of air before the pull of gravity and wind resistance strike a balance. In the case of a human body, he knew, terminal was roughly a hundred and twenty miles an hour. Straight down. Mere seconds ate up thousands of feet.

The clouds folded about him like whipped cream swallowing a raisin. But they weren't so pretty as they had been from nearly a mile above. They were dark gray, damp, slimy against his face.

He broke through and watched the shadowed landscape rush upward to meet him as the plunge continued. His fingers were curved talons on the emergency rip cord, but they made no movement.

Then the preset device, its heart a tiny altimeter, triggered the backpack. The parachute flung heavenward like a small, white explosion.

Jim endured that empty second. Then the chute opened with a crack of sound. The harness snapped him up short just as he was beginning to make out individual trees on the earth below.

He reached up and worked the taut shroud lines to stop the slight back and forth pitching of his body in the harness.

His descent steadied. He dropped with the speed of an express elevator and struck in a stubble-grown field with his knees flexed. The impact jarred him off balance. He tripped and fell on his left side. The parachute immediately began to collapse, settling like an uncertain ghost to earth that had been blasted by centuries of scorching sun.

Jim flipped to his feet and peeled off the harness. He gathered in shroud lines and canopy, making them into a bundle under his left arm.

With his right hand, he unzippered a pocket of his jumpsuit, took out a small light, and winked it three times.

In a few moments he saw the shadows of Willy, Rollin, and Barney converging on him from various directions across the field. Then he let himself have the luxury of a long, exhaled breath. Everybody was down—in one piece.

Willy was the first to reach him. He had a big grin on his face as he rushed up. "What do you know? I licked it! The old stomach didn't turn over once."

Jim slapped him on the shoulder. "Fine." He tucked the light back into his pocket. There was just enough moonlight for them to make out their surroundings. "Anybody spot the equipment chute?"

"I got it on its way okay," Willy said.

"That's right." Barney was breathing faster than normal from his run across the field. "I glimpsed the equipment chute as it opened."

"No breeze," Rollin added. "It couldn't have drifted far."

"A lonely shepherd or peasant farmer might have spotted us," Jim reminded them. "We haven't got all night to look—and we're dead without that equipment pack."

The four broke apart and scattered over the dry, stubbled field. Jim's feet pumped in a tireless trot. His eyes stabbed the shadows in all directions. He had moved a hundred yards without seeing the telltale splash of white that would mark the equipment parachute, when Barney's low but cutting tone carried to him.

"Over here. . . ." Barney's voice came from a direction east of Jim. "Tangled in a dead fig tree. Hurry and give me a hand, you other three Jonahs in the belly of the whale!"

3. A SPECIALIST

FROM THE WINDOW of his private jet Captain Stefan Zovoloff watched the sparkling Mediterranean wash the shores of Masacar far below. The morning sunlight reflected hotly from the beaches. Here and there fishing villages clustered. They looked quaint from this high altitude. They looked as if life amid the mud-brick huts, with long afternoon siestas and evenings of community dancing about a bonfire, would appeal to a lazy man.

Zovoloff knew just how wrong the picture was. Life down there was grim and hard. A few flimsy fishing boats had stretched their tattered sails and moved dangerously far in desperate search for a catch. The

fishing grounds along this coast weren't good, and
Zovoloff wondered idly and without pity how many
children would cry for more fishhead stew tonight.

The landscape unfolding for miles ahead was
dreary. The low, rolling dunes of dull brown looked as
if countless centuries of merciless sun had roasted the
last ounce of life from them. This picture, Zovoloff
knew, was almost literally true. The peasant's child
would be lucky tonight if he got a gristle of mutton
in his soup.

Zovoloff wondered if the people down there saw
the irony of their lot. The peasant didn't abandon the
land, or the fisherman his nets, simply because there
was no escape in Masacar. Both lived in the shadow
of the same poverty.

Zovoloff hoped his business here wouldn't take
long. The stories he'd heard about the fabulous presidential palace didn't interest him much. He'd seen
the sights, all the way from the Taj Mahal to the Em-
pire State Building. He couldn't abide this dreary land
below. He wanted to get the business done and hurry
back to his reward.

His flinty eyes sparked. The prospects for the
future were indeed exciting. Success on this mission
would mean a promotion to full colonel. The higher
rank carried with it privileges reserved for the ruling
elite in Zovoloff's part of the world. A summer dacha
on the Black Sea. A luxurious motorcar, with private
chauffeur. Choice food. Tailored clothing. His own
box at the theater.

The important nature of his mission might well put

his name in the history books. Colonel . . . but why
stop there? Once a man was in the jealously limited
higher ranks, he could keep right on rising—if he had
the cunning to play his rivals off against each other.

General.

What a nice taste the word left in the mouth!

General Stefan Zovoloff, the man who made the
Belorra process available only to the right-thinking
revolutionary masses.

Who could tell? The state rewrote history to fit its
own best interests. By the time the future books were
written, the name of the traitorous, reactionary
Belorra might have been wiped away. Some day the
whole process might be known as the Zovoloff method
for synthesizing basic food.

But Zovoloff was too hardheaded to forget the present moment for very long. Right now he was but a
captain on the most important mission of his career,
with a problem named Janar Aqaban.

He would have to more than match Aqaban in
cunning if he were to strike a bargain that would
please his superiors. They were foxy thieves, these
Aqabans, big for their britches and puffed up with
self-importance. Small men at heart, when they got
their claws on a tiny, pitiable nation, they strutted like
world conquerors.

But we need them, Zovoloff admitted, the despi-
cable men who will sell out their own people and
institutions. Once the puppets are in our grip we can
decide whether or not they are dancing the tune to
our like—or if they should be sent on a Siberian vaca-

tion. Zovoloff smiled to himself in satisfaction.

The jet slowed with the sensation that it had slipped through an invisible wall. Zovoloff came out of his musings with a start. The warning light over the door to the pilot's cabin had turned on. Zovoloff reached for his safety belt and fastened it quickly.

The earth below had changed its character. It was now dotted with patches of green, date groves, grazing sheep like small white blankets on a few hillsides.

The city of Masarium slid into view as the plane began to lose altitude in a long, shallow bank.

Zovoloff craned his short, powerful neck as he pressed his face close to the window. He studied the city below as he might an anthill.

The streets on the outskirts were like trails cut by wiggle-worms through clusters and rows of huts. The people were black specks—children gazing skyward at the airplane, women trudging to the public wells with water jugs on their heads, a farmer driving a string of donkeys toward the marketplace.

Downtown Masarium attempted to look modern. There were a few blocks of stores, shops, hotels, parks, broad avenues, office buildings. A few cars and lumbering buses stirred little ribbons of dust from pavings that were continually filmed by the sandy breath of the desert.

Zovoloff's gaze lingered longest on the presidential palace. Even he was impressed. The compound covered an area as large as a dozen city blocks. The bygone caliphs had squandered lavishly on their fortress. The palace itself was like a three-dimensional picture from the Arabian Nights. It was built of slabs of polished limestone and marble dragged in by thousands of slaves. But, despite its massive proportions, it gave Zovoloff the impression of being light and airy. The windows were tall, graceful arches, the porticoes shadowed, the spires and minarets delicately thrusting toward the heavens.

The grounds were like a lush, tropical park. The gardens reflected every brilliant color. The twining walkways were shaded by tall palms and bowers of broad-leafed vines. Surrounded by a glistening pool, a fountain shot a rainbow spray.

The layout was shielded from vulgar eyes—and enemies—by a thick, high wall of stone. The palace, Zovoloff conceded, looked as impregnable as . . . well, the Kremlin.

As the aircraft flashed past, Zovoloff glimpsed the scars which diggers had made near the palace walls. The archaeological project, Zovoloff knew, had been started when the previous government opened the ancient site to a team of American, British, and West German scientists. The site had proved out well. Much had been learned about the migrations and wars of ancient peoples. Museums and private collectors had bid avidly for unearthed statuettes, pottery, and tools from the Bronze and Early Iron Ages. The government had used the money to start an irrigation project in southern Masacar.

Then Aqaban had taken over. As soon as he had felt somewhat secure in the seat of power, he had deported the Western archaeologists and stopped the irrigation project. But he had continued the diggings —with absolute control over the proceeds.

Zovoloff mused on the strange workings of the world. How had a man like Aqaban rated so much good fortune? He had hit a jackpot in a land too poor to feed itself. Art treasures which had been buried for centuries had fallen into his hands. But these treasures were nothing compared to the biggest prize—the formula the traitorous upstart had wrenched from Dr. Hasman Belorra.

It was all too much.

Zovoloff's chain of thought broke as he felt the first squealing touch of the wheels. The airplane settled on the runway. Distant, scraggly palm trees flashed past. The speed slackened. The plane rolled to a stop. The pilot revved the engines lightly, turned the craft, and taxied toward the hangars and the dusty, Mediterranean-style administration building.

The airport, Zovoloff recalled, had been built by the earlier government—with American aid. It had brought in a flow of tourist dollars. But Aqaban's regime had scared away vacationers, and now a hint of creeping decay lay over the buildings and two bisecting runways.

The plane eased to a stop, its twin jets dying with a whisper. Both the pilot and copilot came out of their cabin. They were burly, bullet-headed men whose training wasn't limited to flying skill. If the occasion arose, they could carry out any order from Zovoloff with deadly efficiency.

The copilot paused beside the seat as Zovoloff

unsnapped his safety belt. The pilot moved on to open the cabin door.

"I'll attend to the luggage, Captain," the copilot said.

Zovoloff nodded. The contents of his large attaché case and two suitcases included a small transmitter tuned to the same frequency as a receiver in the cabin of the plane.

"I want both of you to stay with the aircraft constantly," Zovoloff said. "If anything goes haywire, our slippery friend might arrange an accident to keep us from getting off the ground. I hope you won't be too uncomfortable."

"Not at all, Captain. The two of us will make out nicely, with our own company and the comforts of the aircraft."

Zovoloff took a final glance out the window as he rose from his seat. Two big, black cars were parked in front of the administration building. Zovoloff guessed that the Mercedes limousine with the bulletproof windows was Aqaban's personal car. The official welcoming party, a dozen men dressed in fawn-colored uniforms liberally splashed with gold braid, was moving toward the airplane.

With a thin, cool smile, Zovoloff walked to the cabin doorway. He blinked as sunlight struck his icy blue eyes. He stood a moment, his powerful figure clad in a quiet, dark blue business suit, his short-cropped, bristling brown hair uncovered.

Two airport attendants had wheeled up the portable steps. Zovoloff walked down slowly. Aqaban sprang forward with a smile of greeting. His spotless white uniform outshone all the rest.

"Welcome to Masacar, Comrade Zovoloff!" The greeting was hearty, Aqaban's handshake firm. But Zovoloff suspected that behind the smiling face Aqaban was still a bit miffed. The pipsqueak probably fancied that he should rate at least an ambassador, if not the Party Chief himself.

Zovoloff murmured the expected, "I'm honored to be here. This is a memorable day for both our great nations." Behind his smile was the thought: *You preening wolf, the Party Chief knows what is best.*

The trick in this job, the Chief had explained, was to slip a lone man in and get the Belorra formula out before the Western democracies knew what was going on. Zovoloff's record had dropped the plum in his lap. He was a specialist.

Aqaban's face reminded Zovoloff of a preying eagle's. But Zovoloff knew how to soothe the feathers.

"The President of the Presidium sends his greetings," Zovoloff said. "He is looking forward to the pleasure of talking to you face to face. Meanwhile, he requests that you accept me as his personal representative. Be assured that you are dealing with the Party Chief himself."

Aqaban's smile became less strained.

Zovoloff quickly noted the effect of his flattery. He added, "Two heads of state could not very well meet on this occasion without the imperialists wondering what was going on. The Party Chief was certain that a man of your intelligence would see this instantly."

"Of course." Aqaban's chest swelled. "Did he mention when he might like to hold a summit conference?"

Summit? With you attending? Zovoloff thought.

"He is as eager as you," Zovoloff said aloud.

Aqaban's eyes glinted with satisfaction. Inwardly, Zovoloff glowed with the same feeling. He had started off on the right foot with this fellow. Already he sensed swift success.

Aqaban introduced the officials who had pressed forward but remained obediently silent until now. Zovoloff smiled and shook hands with the commanding general of Aqaban's cutthroat army, the Masacarian minister of the interior, the minister of state, and several lesser officials.

Zovoloff gave each a quick, penetrating study and filed them in his mind.

The party strolled toward the parked cars, Zovoloff and Aqaban in the lead. Aqaban chatted affably, inquiring if Zovoloff's trip had been comfortable, if the good weather had held all the way across the sea.

The two settled in the rear seat of the limousine. Zovoloff was pressed back against the seat as the driver started the car and shot it from the administration building.

Aqaban guffawed. "He always drives like this, Comrade. On my orders. I like to feel the power of the car, the speed."

Zovoloff hung onto the strap beside the window. He accepted the wild ride as part of the job. But the pell-mell rush over ruts and potholes seemed ridiculous to him.

The car whisked past brown fields where farmers plowed with oxen and labored under shoulder poles with buckets of water for feeble irrigation. As they zoomed into the outskirts of the city, the dreary hovels were closer together. Tattered children stared from barren, hard-packed yards.

The streets had been cleared all the way to the palace, and the car slowed only when it wended its way through the archaeological diggings. Zovoloff glanced at the work. Men were toiling with picks, shovels, wheelbarrows. Trenches and terraces had been cut down to levels that probably dated back two thousand years. Perhaps in that distant past a Roman conspirator had ridden chariot or litter over this very spot, on his way to deal with a remote ancestor of Aqaban.

The shadow of the palace wall soon swallowed the car. The limousine slammed to a stop with its nose almost touching a ponderous, steel-barred gate.

On either side were concrete and steel pillboxes. In fawn-colored uniforms and polished black boots, Aqaban's elite guardsmen stood at attention with automatic weapons in the crooks of their arms. They snapped salutes. One clicked his heels and turned to a steel-encased call box embedded in the wall. He keyed open the box and spoke into the communicator.

The gate lifted and the car glided through. Zovoloff had the sensation that he had been wafted magically from Masacar into a lovely foreign country. The glimpse from the air had been but a hint of the beauty of the palace and grounds.

The Mercedes hummed along an avenue lined with flower gardens, lush lawns, tall palms, spreading umbrella trees.

The approach encircled a vast courtyard graced with marble columns and statues. Towering beyond the court, the extended wings of the palace reflected a pink glow from the sun.

The car stopped in front of the wide, shallow marble stairs leading to the arched front entrance.

Aqaban sprang from the car with a droll laugh. "Welcome to my humble hut, Comrade!"

The remark brought a small smile to Zovoloff's face. He walked beside Aqaban, up the steps and into an enormous entry hall. The curved ceiling was no less than three stories high. Niches in the walls held relics of earlier days—medieval armor, shields, crossed swords and lances. An indoor fountain directly ahead splashed a soothing murmur. In the pool at the fountain's base were giant goldfish.

"I think you will find your quarters to your liking," Aqaban said. He snapped his fingers at the four hovering servants who had appeared. "Show Comrade Zovoloff. . . ."

"I'm really not tired," Zovoloff interrupted. "Why don't you first show me our prize?"

"Dr. Belorra's *my* prize." Aqaban tried to soften the words with a chuckle. "That is, until we have settled some details."

"Naturally." Zovoloff wasn't able to keep the stiffness entirely from his voice. "But I'm sure you understand. I've come a long way to see this man."

Aqaban threw his arm about Zovoloff's shoulder, trying a little too hard to be friendly.

"Comrade," Aqaban implored, "please don't doubt. I have exactly what I said I had—the man and the formula. And the man is in one piece, very much so, as you will see. Come along, I will show you."

4. THE FAVORITE VISITOR

DR. BELORRA heard the echoes of clicking footsteps from far down the corridor. They were heading toward his dungeon-like cell, he realized.

The sound snapped him back to his grim surroundings. His mind had been far away, his thoughts concerned with a lithium isotope's behavior under certain electronic potentials.

He stopped his pacing and stared at the age-crusted sheet-iron door. He recognized the sharp snapping of Janar Aqaban's heels. He had heard the sound often enough, when Aqaban had strutted back and forth during the long hours of questioning.

Dr. Belorra's muscles tightened as he waited for

the footsteps to pause outside his quarters.

The solitary cell, about eight by ten feet, seemed to close in a little. Dr. Belorra knew it was somewhere in the west wing of the palace, in that old security section where caliphs had once imprisoned their most dangerous enemies.

Directly behind Dr. Belorra was the room's single window, a high, narrow slit with steel bars set in the stone at intervals of six inches. The window offered a small, tantalizing view of lovely gardens and a splash of open, blue sky. Too many hours at the window would have wrecked a man.

The cell was mostly underground. This—and the tropical climate—caused the walls to sweat and mildew. The fungus continuously whitewashed the walls with a chalky slime.

At first the smell and the dankness had been more than an irritation. Dr. Belorra's prison clothing, rough brown cotton trousers and shirt, had clung noisomely to his flesh. His body had been damp and itchy. But he had gradually grown accustomed to the unpleasantness.

He had landed in the cell without quite realizing how he had survived the shattering ordeals that had hit him one after another—the whispered warning by a friend that he must leave his house and laboratory while he still had time ... the flight through the back streets of Masarium ... across the open countryside ... his realization that both he and Miriam couldn't make the border ... the argument they had had ... the tears in her eyes as she had finally accepted his command to split up . . . the thirst and bone-crushing tiredness that had carried him southward toward the oasis at Tell-Ikano . . . his stumbling, half-dead arrival—only to find the minions of Janar Aqaban waiting.

They had returned him to Masarium, to the white lights in his eyes, to the endless hours of questions, to the truth drugs.

He had hung on, telling himself that Miriam was safe. But he couldn't be sure of this. She might be under lock and key just down the corridor.

When they put him in the cell, he knew that this solitary confinement might be Aqaban's most effective weapon. He'd slept. Dreamed. Awakened in a sweat. He had paced the cramped space to exercise. In the dank silence the sound of his own footsteps had become little spikes driving into his mind.

He had glared at the slimy walls. How could he break the power of the moldering trap? If only he had a tool to busy his hand, a book to occupy his mind.

Then inspiration had crept in. His shoulders had stiffened. He had shuffled to the wall, lifted his hand, and made a short mark in the mildew with his finger-tip.

A laugh had cracked from his throat. At once the blood had felt livelier in his veins. The fungus-whitened walls made a very good writing surface!

With a fresh luster in his red-rimmed eyes, he had thought: *Let's see . . . if an electron, passing through a cloud chamber, is subjected to magnetic deflection X and its primary speed is c-minus-Y. . . .*

Hours later he had covered most of one wall with his calculations. His imaginary scientific problem had been interrupted by a guard bringing dinner.

As he ate black bread and thin barley soup that night, Dr. Belorra had grinned in wolfish satisfaction.

The creeping mildew would blot out his symbols. So much the better. Mother Nature would supply fresh writing surfaces.

Neither did it matter that his mental games might never have a practical application. With his body sealed in stone, his mind could now roam an endless landscape. He had whipped the cell at its own game. . . .

Now the sound of footsteps stopped outside the sheet-iron door. Dr. Belorra waited, a breath drawn in. The heavy bolt outside grated. The door creaked open.

Dr. Belorra's handsome Grecian face settled in determined lines as he wondered what Aqaban now had up his sleeve.

Aqaban hadn't come alone. Close beside him was a powerfully built man dressed quietly in a blue suit. The man didn't reflect the showiness that Aqaban liked to display. But as Dr. Belorra looked at the hard chin, the icy blue eyes, the ridged forehead, and the bristling military-cut brown hair, he sensed an enemy even more ruthless than Aqaban himself.

Aqaban was wearing that taunting smile. "Doctor, meet Captain Stefan Zovoloff. Captain, Dr. Hasman Belorra, our guest for the moment."

With a wry smile Dr. Belorra gave Aqaban tit for

tat. "I'm the favorite visitor in the palace," he returned.

Aqaban's lean, narrow face darkened a shade, but Zovoloff's eyes glinted. He lifted a brow as he studied the impressive figure before him. "You seem to have worn well, Doctor."

"Did you expect a man cringing on his knees?" Dr. Belorra needled a look at Aqaban. "I assure you, Captain Zovoloff, the barley soup is excellent. And, it so happens, barley soup is one of my favorites. I often kept a beaker of it bubbling on a Bunsen burner in my laboratory. It shortened the break for lunch."

Aqaban's face tinged purple. "Maybe we should change your menu, Doctor. How does black bread and water sound?"

"I should thrive on it."

Zovoloff kept himself from laughing at Aqaban. "Quite a papa tiger you've trapped in here, Your Excellency."

"So he thinks!"

"I imagine he gave you quite a chase."

Aqaban took a steadying breath. His instincts were always cautious when he considered speaking the truth. Why tell Zovoloff that Belorra might not have been caught at all—if a desert tribal chief, currying favor, hadn't reported the doctor in the south?

"He wasn't so foxy," Aqaban said. "When he reached the oasis at Tell-Ikano, I had men there, waiting."

"Very clever," Zovoloff remarked.

Aqaban made a small, haughty motion with his

shoulders. "Once I figured he was moving south, I had him. He had to be headed for Tell-Ikano—unless he wanted to die in the desert."

Aqaban glowered at Dr. Belorra. "He took seventy-two straight hours of questioning," Aqaban continued. "He could have saved himself the trouble. I had some of the new truth serum flown in. A country so poor lacks extensive drug supplies—but we have friends outside our borders."

Zovoloff strolled over and looked at the latest mathematical symbols Dr. Belorra had made on the wall.

"What's this, Doctor?"

The man was suspicious of everything, Dr. Belorra thought.

"It's nothing," Dr. Belorra said.

"He plays a game," Aqaban added.

"Some game." Zovoloff's finger stabbed here and there. "He's playing with a lithium isotope in a way I've never seen before."

Zovoloff turned and studied Dr. Belorra for a long moment. Finally he nodded. "Yes, I think you'd be very clever at games, Doctor."

"But he lost," Aqaban said in a pleased tone.

Zovoloff shot him a look. For an instant Zovoloff's eyes were naked, cold with contempt. "He could game with you, Aqaban, and you'd never know it."

Hidden at his side, Aqaban's hand clenched. "What are you suggesting?" His tone was icy.

"Something that should be quite plain," Zovoloff said. "You have a wily, durable papa tiger here."

"So?"

"We'd look quite foolish if it turned out he didn't come across with the real formula, after all."

Aqaban gave a snort of disgust. "How could he help it? Remember—the truth serum."

"Remember also," Zovoloff suggested, "for every attack there is a defense. You must learn to take nothing on faith, Comrade."

Aqaban was almost trembling with rage.

"Would you care to enlighten me, Captain?" Aqaban asked in mock humility. "What's the defense against truth serum?"

"Preparation in advance. He knew you'd get around to using it."

Aqaban's smile had the hint of a sneer. "Don't you imagine he was searched and watched constantly from the moment of his arrest? He had no counter-drug, no chance to take one."

"I'm not talking about a counter-drug," Zovoloff said. He looked directly into Dr. Belorra's dark eyes. "I'm sure you could tell His Excellency what I am talking about."

"I'm not a specialist in truth serums," Dr. Belorra said mildly.

"But you're a scientist. I'm sure the properties of most truth drugs are well enough known to you. *You* wouldn't be surprised by the cases on record where men have beaten truth drugs."

Aqaban was chafing to know the meaning of what Zovoloff was driving at, but he didn't want to show his ignorance. He stepped forward and lifted his hand as if he would slap Dr. Belorra.

"Speak when you're spoken to! Answer the captain!"

Dr. Belorra looked at the upraised hand. His lips thinned. He said nothing.

Aqaban dropped his hand and stood slapping his thigh, as if that had been his intention all along.

"I would guess that the captain," Dr. Belorra said after a moment, "is suggesting that a man can use hypnosis to beat many truth serums. He can sometimes hide a fact from the drugs by substituting a phony answer in advance—while he is under hypnosis. Later, under the drug, his subconscious mind responds with the phony answer, not the real fact you're after. Is that about it, Captain?"

"I couldn't have put it neater myself," Zovoloff said.

"B-But I know I have the formula!" Aqaban spluttered. "Who would have hypnotized him and prepared him in advance?"

"Perhaps his daughter," Zovoloff said. "After all, she has been steeped in a scientific atmosphere from the day she was born. She would have no trouble learning enough of simple hypnotic technique to pull the trick off."

"But he was alone when we caught him!" Aqaban was sweating with the effort to collect himself. Everything had seemed so sure—now this unexpected turn. . . .

"Not from the time they took to their heels," Zovoloff said. "They had plenty of time together. Too bad you let Miriam Belorra slip through your fingers."

Dr. Belorra had a breathless moment. Then a rush

of feeling filled his throat. His eyes blurred. Miriam
had made it—she had gotten out of Masarium!

His knees were suddenly limp. But it was a wonder-
ful feeling. He sank to the edge of the hard, wooden
cot, his mind whirling.

Miriam, he knew, wouldn't broadcast all that had
happened in Masacar. If she did, an international
furor might trigger Aqaban to final action against her
father. She would certainly try for a contact in a
friendly government.

Zovoloff took a menacing step toward Dr. Belorra.
"Before you shout with joy, Doctor, let me tell you
one thing. We're not as bungling as my friend here.
Our people have picked up the trail of your daughter.
We've learned that Miriam Belorra is in Rome. All
that remains now is for us to pinpoint the location—
and smuggle her out of the country."

Dr. Belorra flinched. Rome . . . of course. He and
Miriam had visited the Eternal City twice in years
past, once when he lectured at the university, again
during one of their rare vacations. Top scientific circles had made his welcome royal. He had formed
several lasting friendships in Rome. Miriam would
have considerable influence there.

"We'll perhaps let you lunch together," Zovoloff
said icily, "when she is in our hands."

Zovoloff nodded to Aqaban that he was ready to
leave. Visibly upset by the developments of the past
minutes, the dictator threw a final glare at Dr. Belorra. He followed Zovoloff out, and the sheet-iron
door closed. The bolt went home with a clang that

resounded in the corridor.

Feeling suddenly drained and exhausted, Dr. Belorra fell back on the cot. His staring eyes were fixed on the wet ceiling, but he wasn't actually seeing it. He knew every bump, chip, and crack in the stone already. He could predict how many minutes it would take for the moisture to gather in the next heavy drop and fall.

He thought of Miriam in Rome—where she wasn't so safe, after all.

His eyes closed heavily. Zovoloff's scheme was clear. Dr. Belorra didn't know if he could resist. They could get to him through Miriam. She was the hostage Zovoloff and his crowd needed to pick the Belorrian brains for a long time to come. . . .

As they walked along an ornate tapestried hallway on the second floor, Aqaban and Zovoloff were also thinking of Miriam Belorra.

Aqaban mentally kicked himself. Zovoloff was using the girl's escape as a tool to strengthen his position. Aqaban's mind seethed with dire proposals for the inept lackeys who'd let the girl slip through their fingers.

Behind the mask of his face, Zovoloff was a lot more uncertain and anxious than he appeared. He was eager for news from Rome. The girl had already proven her cleverness in shaking pursuit—and by now she had had ample time to make a friendly contact.

Aqaban paused at a tall, hand-carved door. His growing diffidence was invisible behind a wreathing smile. "I believe you will like the suite, Comrade," he murmured.

He flung open the door with a flourish. The quarters beyond were indeed sumptuous. The walls of the large sitting room were decorated with soft-toned, restful landscape murals. The curved ceiling supported a chandelier that was like dripping diamonds. The pale green carpeting looked ankle deep. Deep, velvet-covered couches and chairs made soothing promises of comfort. A long, low table with ivory legs and a polished marble top held a buffet of exotic foods and tropical fruits.

Zovoloff strolled in. Across the room tall French doors were framed in draperies of pale white raw silk. Beyond, Zovoloff saw a small, elevated terrace with chaise longues and potted palms. To his left, double doors stood open on a bedroom. Zovoloff glimpsed a massive four-poster, silk-canopied bed.

"The quarters are very nice." Zovoloff nodded. He seemed pleased, mollified. "Comrade . . . I suppose you did your best. At least, you got hold of Belorra."

"Frankly, I hadn't worried too much about the girl —until you brought up that fantastic possibility of hypnotism."

"Fantastic, Comrade?"

"Well, after all"—Aqaban shrugged impatiently— "what evidence have you? What put the idea in your head that the formula I have may be bogus, a post-hypnotic suggestion?"

"Evidence too plain to overlook, Comrade. The character of the man. He is a man of surprising durability. Highly original and creative. He would hold out to the end, and develop any tool at hand. Second, the circumstance. He was in flight. He knew exactly what you were after. His strongest wish would be to thwart you, in the event he was captured."

Aqaban paced with jerky steps, his muscles twitching and restless.

He sneaked a glance at Zovoloff. The foreign agent had moved to the table and was apparently studying the food with a sudden hunger.

"We might quickly settle the question about the formula in your possession," Zovoloff suggested blandly.

A cautious frown creased Aqaban's forehead. "How?"

Zovoloff chose a pomegranate from the fruit bowl. "Show it to me—now."

Aqaban's lean chin jutted. So that was Zovoloff's game: to imprint the formula on his photographic memory even before the bargaining began!

"The formula Belorra recited under the drug might be altered only in small, but critical, details," Aqaban evaded.

Zovoloff glanced at him. "My background includes considerable scientific training. You saw it demonstrated when I interpreted the symbols Belorra had made on the cell wall. I can tell how closely his formula deals with protein."

A moment of silence. Zovoloff stood pitching the ruddy pomegranate a few inches into the air. The gesture was extremely annoying to Aqaban.

"You do understand, Comrade," Zovoloff murmured. "When the truth is finally out about the Belorra formula, the international situation could get very sticky. Before I involve my country and its allies, I have to make sure you have the real article to bargain with."

Aqaban's ego and sense of self-importance had struck a reef. An explosion occurred in his eyes. "I'm no scarecrow seeker of alms on a back street in Masarium! Others might enjoy hearing my terms."

Zovoloff looked at the pomegranate as if he had discovered a rotten spot. So his gambit had failed. He tried a new tactic.

He looked at Aqaban with a fresh show of respect in his eyes. "Perhaps the fault is mine. My words read with a meaning I didn't intend."

Aqaban searched for sincerity in Zovoloff's face.

"If the formula isn't authentic," Zovoloff suggested, "we can always take measures later."

"I don't see why not," Aqaban said. He was slowly regaining his composure. He was a little frightened at the way he had let himself threaten Zovoloff. Aqaban reminded himself that the hours and days ahead could be the most important in his life. It wouldn't do to let emotion interfere.

"May I suggest a first order of business?"

"Why not?" Zovoloff couldn't have been friendlier. "What do you wish?"

"Some guarantees—spelled out—for both sides."

Zovoloff nodded slowly as he mulled it over. He strolled across the room. From the French doors he

mused on the colorful gardens below. Suddenly he
detected movement down there. Fawn-colored uniforms. One of them slipped from sight below the
hanging terrace. A thin smile cut Zovoloff's face. The
upstart, he thought, must also have his guards with
listening devices in the room right next to this one.

He turned away from the raw silk draperies. His
face was again bland as he glanced at Aqaban. "Guarantees," he murmured. "Sounds reasonable."

Aqaban took a breath. "I'm glad we agree."

"You have a list of your needs? Armaments? Food?"

Aqaban hesitated. "I have a list. But. . . ."

"But?"

"The situation changes in Masacar every hour."
Aqaban's eyes glinted with greed. "I'll need a few
more planes than I at first thought."

"How about the pilots to fly them?"

"They're being trained," Aqaban said.

Zovoloff was thoughtful. He pulled idly at the lobe
of his left ear. *Once we get the formula,* he thought,
you will number your days, little jackel.

"I think we could add a few more planes," he said.

Aqaban's face glowed. He rubbed his hands together briskly. "Give me tanks, guns, planes, and
bullets to keep the rabble in its place and you'll find
I can match your generosity. Belorra, his daughter,
the formula . . . you can have the lot."

Zovoloff's eyes hooded. Against his lids shimmered
the vision of a full colonel's insignia, the key to privi-
lege, luxury, power. "I had rather counted on that,
Comrade Aqaban," he murmured.

5. AT THE DIGGINGS

As THEY TRUDGED toward the archaeological diggings, Willy Armitage and Barney Collier sized up each other. They were dressed as peasants of the region, in sandals, pantaloons, jerkins, and turbans. The clothing was tattered and grimy.

"Looks like we haven't had anything else to put on our backs for weeks," Barney said.

"Smells like it, too." Willy held his nose. "I wonder where Phelps dug up these rags. A wonder they didn't spoil everything in the equipment pack."

"You'll enjoy the smell if we run into a close inspection." The dust made puffs beneath Barney's feet.

"Think we'll pass?"

"You'd better believe it."

"If we don't . . ." Willy began.

". . . we'll see the inside of Janar Aqaban's dungeon a lot sooner than scheduled," Barney finished for him.

"Did you have to say it?" Willy growled. "I'd rather not see it at all. I wish there was some other way."

"Don't we all?" Barney said. "But Dr. Belorra is in. We're out. If he is to go out, we have to go in. It adds, like simple arithmetic."

"I never did like numbers," Willy grumbled.

They broke off as they neared the edge of the diggings. The ground under their feet now was soft. It was dirt that had been sifted and carted out from the cuts, trenches, and terraces.

They climbed the low mound. In the near distance the glaring white of the palace wall was a backdrop for the scene of activity before them.

Willy whistled softly. "They've sure turned up a lot of ground. Acres of it, and the trenches and terraces all so neat."

The diggers were small figures working within fifty yards of the palace wall. They were widening a deep trench to form a terrace. Some were out of sight below ground level. Others raised and lowered mattocks and shovels with tired efforts. A thin, weary line of them was pushing loaded wheelbarrows several yards to a dumping area.

"Get a load of the boss," Willy said. "That must be him under the one palm tree in sight."

In the scraggly patch of shade, the overseer stretched and stood up. He was a beefy, swarthy man.

He wore duck pants, a shirt open halfway down the front over his huge chest, a floppy, wide-brimmed straw hat. He had a bandolier crossing his left shoulder to his right side, where a heavy pistol hung.

He hadn't yet spotted Willy and Barney. He scratched his prickly growth of black beard. "Come on, you lazy camels," he bellowed at the diggers. "Show me something besides dirt—at least a bit of pottery. Will you get your rations for merely making holes in the ground?"

"Sounds like the site is playing out," Willy said behind his hand.

"What else? Janar Aqaban chased off most of the trained people," Barney whispered. "A good archaeologist reads the surface for clues where to plant a pick and shovel. The birds Aqaban has put in charge have got a political plum—but not the know-how. They're wasting the work crew to rut the ground like blind pigs just hoping to find an acorn."

"From their attitude I'd bet they're not even hoping to find that."

"Can you blame them?" Barney asked.

"Nope," Willie said. "But I got a hope. I just hope our briefing on the diggings is dead on the button."

"The information came from the top," Barney reminded him. "From the very archaeologists who opened the site and worked it until Aqaban threw them out."

"Well, okay." Willy sighed. "If anybody could give with the details about this place, it should be them."

Barney's gaze had idled about. To his left, away

from the present work, the ruins of an ancient room were exposed. Twenty feet below the present-day ground level, the stone floor and crumbled walls could be made out. It had been stripped of all artifacts that might bring in money. Already the desert wind was dropping grains of sand to reclaim the room.

Barney let his imagination play. An ancient Roman guard station? Could be. Barney envisioned tough veterans scanning the road to the procurator's residence, their burnished helmets gleaming, short swords at their sides.

Barney grunted as Willy suddenly planted an elbow in his side.

"He's giving us the once-over," Willy whispered. "Ready or not, we start the act. Here we go. . . ."

The overseer was motioning to them with his massive right arm. They moved with dragging feet, picking their way over the rubble.

"You walk like old women, you donkeys!" the overseer yelled. "Hurry it up!"

Barney and Willy picked up the pace as they neared the scraggly palm tree. Barney flicked a look at the workers. The overseer's distraction was all they needed to rest on their shovels.

Hands on hips, the barrel-shaped overseer looked Barney and Willy up and down. At close range, the overseer's face looked like a potato oiled with sweat. His eyes were the purple of grapes. They had a mischievous glint, and they weren't entirely unfriendly. Barney sensed that the big man, in a different time and place, might have been a deckhand on a tramp steamer, or even a roustabout with a circus.

"What are you hanging around here for?" the overseer boomed.

"We're hungry," Willy pleaded.

The overseer's face hardened. It seemed deliberate, as if he had to make an effort. "You and how many others! Where do you come from?"

Barney lifted his arm and pointed. "From the south," he said truthfully.

"You left withering fields and bleating, dying flocks behind, I suppose."

"We didn't have any flocks," Willy said, "just the work we can do with our hands and brains."

"Bah! The lot of you . . . I suppose you want to complain about the irrigation project being stopped."

"Would it do any good?" Barney asked.

The overseer glared. Then tiredness slipped into the purple eyes. "Don't you realize what our leader is trying to do for you? We have to make our nation strong"—his lips curled scornfully about the words— "so that imperialists and counter-revolutionaries can't return and cheat the people!" He spat on the ground. "I guess you want a job?"

"A job—even at risk of our lives," Barney said.

"Oh, ho! Brave words. But would you risk a callous from the end of a shovel?"

"Give us a chance," Willy said. "We'll show you how to put some muscle in the work."

The overseer's eyes flicked toward the idling crew scattered about. "It's late. But set a pace for these lazy camels, and you shall have a meal."

"Thank you, Excellency!" Barney made a short bow.

"Watch the dirt fly," Willy said.

The overseer waggled a thick finger. "But with care. You have to watch for the tiniest bit of pottery or a broken arrowhead."

"We have the eyes of eagles," Barney said.

"You'd better have! The penalties around here are rough. Anyone who misses a clue to a fresh find— he is a traitor to the state!" The overseer thumbed sweat from his lumpy forehead. "Now get your shovels from the cart over there. And the rest of you," he roared out, "get to work."

Willy and Barney walked to the two-wheeled cart. Its donkey was browsing in a brown, strawlike clump a few yards away.

The IMF pair crossed their shoulders with shovels and walked to the edge of the terrace. They dropped down among the listless line of diggers and plunged their shovels into the dirt which the mattock wielders had loosened.

Their energy brought dark looks and mutterings.

"You fools must still believe the fairy tales," the digger behind Barney hissed. "Slow it down!"

"You, over there!" the overseer yelled. "Save your breath for digging."

The remaining hours of the afternoon slipped away in a haze of sweat and shovels biting into the earth.

At last the overseer called out, "All right, you worms. You can now partake of our glorious leader's generosity."

Willy and Barney straightened, pressing kinks out of their backs with their palms. Their jerkins and pantaloons were blackened with sweat and dirt.

They crawled out of the trench and joined the workers streaming toward the cart where the shovels were deposited. Everyone was now moving with more spirit than they had all day.

A dusty pickup truck, burdened with a huge tub of stew, had arrived. The smell of simmering leeks, garlic, and barley brought a growling response from Willy's stomach. He and Barney jostled into the line forming behind the truck.

The driver got out of the cab, unhooked the tail gate, and started the mess line. The overseer strolled over to talk with him while the men were being fed. Each man was handed a tin plate, into which a ladle of stew was splashed. A chunk of black bread was added to the meal. As soon as each worker had his ration, he hurried to the nearest spot he could find to sit down and devour the food. The men were soon hunkered figures scattered all about the truck.

Sitting on a stone, plate on his knees, Willy watched the men eat. Hungry as he was, he wished he could share his food without arousing suspicion. He could afford to miss a meal. These fellows couldn't.

Barney eased down beside Willy. His eyes were also troubled as he studied the ravenous workers.

"Rather points up our mission, doesn't it?" Barney muttered. "People so wretchedly hungry. . . ."

Willy nodded. "I'm glad Phelps picked me for this one, all right."

The brief desert twilight settled while the men were eating. When they had finished, they drifted slowly from the diggings. Some would return to mud-brick huts filled with hungry children. Others would seek any place to sleep—a sheltered spot in an alley, a building doorway.

Willy and Barney ambled southward. They looked as though they were headed for a ghetto area more than two miles distant.

Full darkness had swept over the earth when they arrived at the extremities where the archaeologists had first started the diggings.

They sat down as if to rest on a low mound the desert winds were already wearing smooth. Far off to their right, the lights of downtown Masarium cast a low haze into the sky. A few degrees left, the minarets of the palace stood golden in the splash of floodlights.

Between the IMF pair and the distant minarets nothing seemed to move. The pickup had departed. The diggings lay silent.

Willy and Barney slipped from the mound into the shallow trench at its base. They continued to wait, ears straining, eyes staring over the trench lip. Almost an hour passed before they were satisfied.

"Okay," Willy whispered, "we've got it all to ourselves for a while."

"Use the minarets for a beacon," Barney said, "and we'll hit the spot where we were digging today head-on."

They eased out of the trench and started the long

belly-crawl back. They were invisible from half a dozen paces away. Now and then a clicking pebble marked their presence. A rattle in a dead thicket froze them. A small black shadow rustled toward the sky.

"Stupid bird," Willy muttered. "Doesn't he know birds are supposed to fly in daytime?"

He inched along behind Barney. Long minutes passed. Then they were near the terrace where they had dug during the afternoon. Willy heard a thin spill of dirt as Barney veered into a trench.

He crawled down beside Barney. The raw earth about them felt cooler, more moist, than it had during the slavish day.

There was a soft rustle as Barney slid the small map from his pantaloons. Phelps had sketched the diagram while he'd talked on overseas telephone to the archaeologists who had worked the site until Aqaban's deportation order.

A tiny, shaded light shed a firefly glow over the map.

"The new trenches and cuts have changed the face of things. So it's a good thing we had plenty of time to sort the layout this afternoon," Barney mused.

Hunkered with his shoulder pressing Barney's, Willy whispered, "The terrace we worked today is about a dozen yards away. Over there." He motioned leftward with his head. "We're after one of the last ones the Western team opened before Aqaban gave them the boot. It should be. . . ." His grubby finger was faintly visible as he traced a line on the paper. "Holy toledo! We're in it!"

Barney's teeth glinted. "How's that for dead reckoning?"

"Man," Willie gulped in amazement, "you could navigate for homing pigeons." Then his teeth clicked. "Uh-uh," he added, "I'm wise to you, pal. You unrolled that map inside your gray matter the minute we got here. You studied the layout and had the target trench picked out even before work knocked off. Then you dropped yourself a landmark you could find in the dark—a stone or a stick in the ground."

"Knock it off." Barney grinned. "You want to feast your eyes on the beauties of the palace gardens—or spend the night sitting here figuring out how I do my feats of magic?"

The pinpoint light flipped off. Barney's shadow dissolved, moving in a crouch along the trench. Willy scrambled after him.

They groped twenty yards or more before Barney stopped.

"This should be it," Barney whispered. "Now we put our backs to work again."

A soft clatter of dirt now and then was the only revelation of their presence as they cleared rubble from the bottom of the trench. Willy laid each stone down carefully as Barney handed it back.

They worked tirelessly, muscles oiled with sweat. Every few minutes they paused to listen for sounds of any other presence about the diggings.

At last a jaggedly arched hole yawned in the base of the trench. Barney dropped to his knees and thrust his head and shoulders into the opening. Willy heard the soft snick as Barney turned his light on. Willy crouched beside him while Barney shone the light down the ancient, stone-lined tunnel.

Barney drew his head out, the light turned off.

"We'd better be glad those old Roman governors liked running water and their hot baths," Barney said. "If they hadn't built the aqueduct, we'd have one fat chance of breaching the palace walls."

Willy wasn't too happy about the chance offered by the ancient Roman water main. "We could get hung in there," he muttered. "Or have a hunk cave in behind us."

"Take courage, Willy. Remember that those Roman engineers built to last. Miles of their roads, bridges, and aqueducts are still in use in Europe."

"This one isn't," Willy grumbled.

"It's going to be."

"So who said I needed courage? Lead on," Willy ordered. "And if you find the thing full of snakes, don't panic."

Barney wriggled headfirst through the opening. Willy fished a coil of string from his pantaloons pocket and snubbed the end securely in a crack in the opening. By playing out the string and counting the measured knots as they passed through his fingers, he would know the distances as they moved inside the aqueduct.

Willy crawled inside. Up ahead, he saw the faint glow of Barney's light. Willy inched along on hands and knees, careful to keep his head down.

Mentally, Willy paid his respects to the fellows who,

two thousand years ago, had cut, fitted, mortared, and joined the stone. It must have brought water from a spring or well that had long since dried up, he surmised. Then they had had to make the duct watertight. Otherwise, seepage would have afflicted the procurator's residence with a case of dry plumbing.

In the dry, desert climate, the tunnel had remained intact. But it was cramped, and the air was dead, foul. The farther he sweated along, the less Willy complimented the builders.

Barney had stopped. Willy drew up close behind. Barney flicked his light over the arched walls and top immediately ahead.

"Easy," Barney said. "We'd better flatten, stretch out, and inchworm it for a few yards. A stone arch is immune to just about anything short of an earthquake, so long as the keystone isn't disturbed. But a couple of places have a loose look I don't like. We won't chance brushing them with our shoulders."

Willy pressed the string between his thumb and forefinger. "We're ninety-seven yards in," he reported. Like Barney's, his softly spoken words had a sepulchral echo.

"Good. More than halfway."

The crawl continued. The tunnel became suffocating. Willy itched. His elbows and knees had been rubbed raw. Bit by bit the string uncoiled from about his hand. Then, as a knot bumped between his fingers, he said with a gateful sigh, "Two hundred and sixteen yards. We're inside the palace wall."

They stopped and rested a moment. How far ahead

the tunnel continued, they didn't know.

Barney squirmed about. His fingers parted a side seam in his pantaloons. His hand disappeared in the small opening. He grimaced as he ripped a wide swathe of adhesive tape from his thigh. His hand came out holding what appeared to be a narrow piece of metal. As he unfolded it, the metal became a knifelike tool.

He studied the stone about him, then handed Willy the light. The tip of the tool made a steady, soft snicking sound as it cut away at the mortar.

Lying on his side, Barney worked the block of stone loose, inserting the tool at one end and then the other. Barney handed the tool to Willy. Both held their breaths as Barney took hold of the stone and eased it free.

"Whew!" Willy exclaimed.

Barney forearmed clammy sweat from his face. "It's going to work out just as we figured. We can cut out this trace without disturbing the adjoining stones. Then we can shove the rubble on ahead in the tunnel, and have plenty of room to work to the surface."

Willy had to hold the light, wait, and watch while Barney removed the stones with the precision of a jeweler. He was set to drag Barney back at the first hint of a cave-in. He wished he were doing the digging himself.

Then the section of stones was a jumbled pile in the tunnel beyond, and Barney was burrowing upward. As the earth trickled down he shoved it aside with his feet.

Soon he was visible to Willy only from the waist down. His whisper floated back. "I've struck the tough, viney roots of grass and shrubs."

Willy felt dizzy from the waiting. It was Barney's job now to set his several-jointed tool at a steep outward angle and cut out a small circle of sod. The section could then be lifted and lowered as a trapdoor. Then the metal tool would serve its last purpose. Folded in the shape of a triangle, it would act as a stout brace under the sod.

Their calculations had placed the trapdoor near the inner side of the palace wall, between the wall and a long stand of flowering shrubs. At that shielded location a man's chances of slipping undetected into the palace grounds were excellent.

Barney's knees were bending. He wriggled down into the tunnel with contortive squeezings of his lean body. Willy backed up, giving Barney room.

"Well?" Willy said, his voice filled with impatience.

Barney's sweaty, dirt-crusted face cracked in a smile. "Works like it had greased hinges. I sneaked a look to make sure we'd hit point zero. Couldn't see much of the palace because of the shrubbery. But what a place!"

"We've still got to hide our entrance in the diggings with some loose rubble," Willy reminded. "Let's get a move on."

"Time?"

Willy looked at the luminous watch on his thick wrist. "Almost four A.M."

"We've plenty of time. A good night's work."

They were familiar with the aqueduct now, and the crawl back seemed shorter and easier.

Then, as they emerged in the diggings, Willy heard the thud of a lifted stone being dropped. He reached and cautioned Barney with a touch. They crouched in the concealment of the trench, straining their ears.

They heard a man give a grunt, then the stony rattling of rubble being moved.

Willy inched up the side of the trench. He felt Barney's presence beside him. The hairs on the back of Willy's neck became pricking needles. He had the sinking feeling that everything had gone too well so far. The whole mission could be blown in the next few seconds.

Willy's head crept up until he could see over the edge of the trench. His eyes strained into the night shadows. A faint diffusion of light from the distant glow of the palace minarets lent a weird, moonscape touch to the scene.

Willy felt Barney's touch on his shoulder. Barney had spotted movement, and in a moment Willy saw it, too, the shadowy bulk of a man about thirty yards away. He was in a fever of activity, his body bending and rising as he cleared a small space of stony rubble. Then he dropped to his knees and began to dig.

The bloblike form stood up. He was thrusting an object about a foot long underneath his shirt. Then he turned and ran with a heavy stride along the edge of the diggings, now and then stumbling as piles of soft dirt tugged at his feet. The floppy, wide-brimmed hat was unmistakable.

As the fleeing figure blended into distant shadows, Willy and Barney matched each other with bursts of released breaths.

"How about that?" Willy exclaimed. "The overseer —or I'm a monkey's uncle!"

"Knocking down on the boss," Barney agreed. "He pilfers a statuette or rare vase when he can, stashes it, comes back for it later."

"He'll end up cooking his own goose—and he seemed like he'd be a halfway happy fellow if he had the chance."

"He's a cool cookie," Barney took issue. "He won't stick his neck out. We'll use him."

Willy cut a glance at the almost invisible brown face beside him. "Use him? How?"

"As a barometer. As long as he's safe, we're cozy. If the boom is lowered on him, we can expect Aqaban to order a general search. He'll have men throwing dirt all over the place to see what else the overseer has planted."

"What do you know." Willy grinned. "Aqaban supplies us with a lookout!"

6.
ARRIVAL
IN MASARIUM

JIM PHELPS had trained himself to fall asleep instantly, whatever the circumstances or discomforts. It was a blessed knack for a man whose job often made sleep available only in thirty-minute snatches.

He had also developed the capacity to awaken with senses fully alert. He did so now, eyes snapping open, mind already functioning.

He heard nothing at first in the gray-dawn stillness. A barren back room in the house that had belonged to Dr. Belorra now sheltered him. He and Rollin Hand had searched the house after they had slipped into Masarium early last evening.

The house had once been a comfortable and gracious habitat. Its tile-roofed wings encompassed a courtyard. Its rooms were large, with tall, beamed ceilings and huge windows. Dr. Belorra's laboratory, study, and library had occupied the west wing.

Little of the former refinement remained, however. Aqaban's vandals had stripped the house of everything that could be carried away. In an orgy of destruction, they had smashed windows and set fire to the west wing. The gardens had quickly gone to weeds. Spiny vines crept up the blackened walls. A foot-long desert lizard came to explore the cool shadows in a corner of what had been the living room.

Nothing here was left to attract Aqaban or his men. The superstitious among the poor gave the place a wide berth, believing it now to be a dwelling for evil and destructive spirits.

Phelps had chosen the location as a temporary base for the Masacarian operation. But as he awakened this first morning, he wondered if the place was as secure as he had judged. Perhaps some among the poor would find squatter's rights more impelling than superstition.

Then Phelps heard Rollin's brief laugh as footsteps approached in the hallway. Jim sat up on the mattress of palm fronds he had made for himself in a corner. He was standing when knuckles beat a coded request on the door. "Come," he said.

The door was flung open, framing Rollin, with the figures of Willy and Barney pressing close behind. All wore elated smiles, although Willy and Barney couldn't have been grubbier if they'd burrowed all the way here from the coast.

Jim's own face burst into a smile. "I take it you characters have a free pass to the flower show on the palace grounds."

"You're cooking on the front burner," Barney said.

"We'll trade you a ticket for some soap and water," Willy offered. "Then for some shut-eye. But first, what's for breakfast?"

"We've a special on the menu this morning," Rollin said. "Bully beef, à la tin can."

Willy made a face, but his words revealed his appetite. "Lead me to it!" he said eagerly.

As the three went out, Jim's face settled in serious lines. He turned and dropped to one knee beside the lightweight aluminum suitcase that nestled against the wall next to his bed. He flipped the latches, opened the case, and took out a spotless white shirt.

He rubbed the stubble on his jaw. Shave it close, he thought. Dust the shoes. Have to be prepared for the next phase.

At ten o'clock Phelps stepped from the glare of morning sunlight into the lobby of the Hotel Ibn Lhaso. He wore a conservative suit of banker's gray, a black fedora, and he carried a Morocco leather attaché case.

In the pre-Aqaban era, the hotel had been a favorite with tourists, especially those from the snow-laden countries of northern Europe. But Jim's observant eyes could now pick out signs of hard times. The potted palms in the rococo lobby were dusty and brownish. The draperies were limp. The glass in the

French doors and windows needed cleaning.

Across the lobby a state-appointed clerk's head drooped in a near doze as he sat behind the horseshoe-shaped desk. Three other people, a lone man and a middle-aged couple, were in the lobby, idly noting Jim's appearance. They sat in three of the big over-stuffed chairs, obviously bored. Probably travelers using Masarium as nothing more than a brief-as-possible way stop, Jim thought to himself. The empty couches and chairs, Jim noticed, showed a worn shine on their plush upholstery.

A startled twitch stirred the clerk in his chair as Jim tapped the desk bell. The clerk reddened, then smiled. He was a clean-cut young man who looked awkward and stiff in his unaccustomed business suit, shirt, and necktie. Jim pegged him as an earnest young man of the farm, fields, out-of-doors, who had followed the revolution for idealistic reasons. He had responded to Aqaban's rousing slogans and fired-up, hypocritical speeches. Now he looked a bit tired, drawn, his eyes much older than his years, as if he was beginning to realize both the truth and the fact that it was already too late for his country to turn back.

"A thousand pardons," he said quickly.

"Forget it." Jim grinned. "A little catnap never hurt anyone."

The clerk turned the register for Jim to sign. Jim picked up the pen on its beaded chain. "I'd like the best suite in the house."

"That would be the penthouse. I . . . ah . . . it hasn't

been occupied for a few days. I'll get a maid up there immediately."

"No hurry. I'll take it for a week, perhaps longer. We'll see. Will Swiss currency in advance do?"

The clerk nodded. He turned the register toward him. "Mr. Jim Phelps. I— You haven't completed the spaces, Mr. Phelps. Where is your residence?"

"The Hotel Ibn Lhaso," Jim said blandly.

"I'm really supposed to see that the forms are complete, Mr. Phelps."

"Okay," Jim said agreeably. He spun the register and wrote in the name of the hotel.

An uneasy frown was crawling between the clerk's large, dark, liquid eyes.

"Mr. Phelps . . . no planes are due in or out of the airport until eleven. When did you arrive?"

"Just now," Phelps said easily. He took a flat wallet from the inner pocket of his jacket, fished out a sheaf of bills, and laid them on the counter. "Please take my charge from this and take care of the remainder in your safe, will you?"

"Mr. Phelps, these forms are supposed to be filled. . . ."

"The form *is* filled out," Jim said with an edge in his voice. "Do your duties include insulting guests? Please show me to my suite."

The clerk resolved his quandary by deciding to pass the buck; Jim saw it in the young man's eyes.

The clerk motioned to a bellhop who had ambled up.

"Show Mr. Phelps to the penthouse, then have one

of the maids freshen up the suite. Luggage, Mr. Phelps?"

"Later," Jim said curtly, brushing past the bellhop to lead the way to the elevator.

A few minutes later, between the bellhop's departure and the arrival of the maid, Jim was alone in the penthouse. The suite warranted appreciation, even with its air of disuse. The sitting room was well-appointed, the bedroom capacious, the bath sporting a marble tub, no less.

But Jim's prowling was restless. How long before the clerk disclaimed responsibility by reporting the suspicious stranger to a superior? Would that one have to report to the next higher-up in a chain of totalitarian red tape? *How long before I get some action,* Jim thought.

A knock sounded on the door as if in answer. Jim hurried across the dusty carpeting and yanked open the door.

It was only the maid, a listless-looking woman of later years with skin like brown paper stretched over sharp bones.

Jim nodded her in with her burden of duster, polishing cloths, and towels.

Then, as he was closing the door, he saw that action was arriving in the person of two men stepping from the elevator.

Jim studied them as they surged toward him. They were short and dark, with the dispassionate faces and eyes of hardened thugs.

Jim stepped into the hallway. They rocked to a

stop, one flanking him on either side.

The one on Jim's left opened his mouth to speak. But Jim spoke first.

"You cats took long enough," he said amiably. "After that bit with the desk clerk"—he glanced at his watch—"I expected you at least three minutes ago. Does His Excellency know how slow some of his people are on the uptake?"

The two gaped at him, then at each other.

Jim snapped his fingers. "Come on! Let's get with it. I want an audience with Janar Aqaban—and I intend to have it pronto!"

"The leader himself?" the man to Jim's right said.

"Better bet your thick skull." Jim's voice was authoritative to the point of insult. "When he hears what I have to say, he may have your hide for not getting me to him quicker."

Neither muscleman had ever faced a situation or individual quite like this. Each looked at the other for help. Both made the decision on the moment.

"We'll take you to our superior, Mr. Phelps. It is his responsibility to give the orders, not ours."

One hour and forty minutes later, two brisk young guards in fawn-colored uniforms ushered Jim into Janar Aqaban's presence.

The dictator was seated at a carved ivory table in a small solarium. He was finishing off a lunch of seafood dainties. The curved bay of windows beside him overlooked a jungle-garden of climbing flowers and banana plants.

The two guards halted Jim in the middle of the

room and clicked their heels.

"This is the man, Excellency," the taller one spoke. "He has been thoroughly searched."

Aqaban dropped his linen napkin beside his plate. He studied Jim with a brooding, eagle-eyed stare. "I've never had such gall reported to me."

"I'm not interested in third-rate bureaucrats and their red tape," Jim said. "What I have to say is for your ears alone."

"You didn't mind taking the risk," Aqaban conceded. "And if you intended to whet my curiosity, you've done that." He leaned back. "Now that you've been passed from one level to another, you'll answer some questions from the top."

"Fully." Jim dropped a pointed glance at the guards. Aqaban hesitated, then gave them a small nod. They clicked their heels smartly, about-faced, and goose-stepped out. Jim knew they would post themselves outside the door, in instant reach of their leader if he raised an alarm.

"All right, Phelps, I don't believe in magic. You appeared—from somewhere. How did you get into Masacar?"

"I was flown in." Jim's tone was matter-of-fact.

"Our air facilities are under close watch. You didn't need an airport. You must have come by helicopter."

"A reasonable guess." Jim smiled.

"When?"

"A few hours ago. I reached you as quickly as I could."

"You slip in," Aqaban mused, "then openly make

your presence known to me." He leaned back as his gaze bored in. "Just what are you, Phelps? Whom do you represent?"

"You might call it an international group interested in profitable economic developments."

"Your credentials?"

"Your men took an attaché case from me," Jim said. "In it you'll find letters of credit from Swiss banks that should impress you as a starter. We'll show you plenty more when the time comes."

"International financial syndicates play only for big stakes." Aqaban thoughtfully sucked a bit of lobster from between his teeth. "What could interest you in a country as small and poor as Masacar?"

"A resource that dwarfs all the oil fields of Arabia," Jim said easily. "The Belorra formula."

Aqaban stared, his face darkening. "Are my secrets broadcast on a worldwide frequency?" he hissed. A sudden suspicion flared in his eyes. He smashed his palm against the tabletop. The exquisite, eggshell-thin dishes clattered. "You've already bought some of my officials! They helped you get into the country!"

"Nonsense—and you know it." Jim shrugged aside the dictator's reaction as if the sparks were merely fireflies. "I've told you how I got in. We can put people anywhere on this planet any time we choose. We don't have to bribe small fry. We deal at the top—and never for peanuts."

Aqaban's glower became a mask of indecision. Clearly, the man before him was a brand-new experience to him.

"May I?" Jim requested. Without waiting for permission, he sat down in a chair across the table from Aqaban.

A second place had been set, no doubt for Zovoloff, Jim thought. He and Rollin had noted the arrival of the jet over Masarium and checked it against a timetable of the few remaining regular flights into Masacar.

Jim poured himself a demitasse from a gleaming silver service. He sipped, then gave an appreciative nod. "Captain Zovoloff shouldn't have begged off lunching with you," he remarked. "He missed out on some excellent coffee."

A hint of dumb wonder flicked through Aqaban's eyes. Then his teeth clicked like a snapping shark's. He gripped the edge of the table. "It isn't always healthy for people to pry so deeply into my affairs."

"Our affairs," Jim amended with a smile. "Yours and mine. And we don't pry, Your Excellency—we investigate. We sift rumor from fact, truth from lies. When a situation shows enough promise, then we act."

Aqaban's mind wrestled. His eyes grew beady. "You would know about Zovoloff . . . if he told you . . . if you work together . . . if this is some kind of a test you're putting me to. . . ."

Jim looked at the hawkish face over the rim of the small cup. "You'll have to make up your own mind about that."

"Yes." Aqaban's breath was a soft hiss. "Zovoloff's statement that he had to check his aircraft seemed an excuse to report to his superiors on the radio. I was certain of that. But now . . . isn't it possible that it could have been part of a trick?"

Good grief, Jim thought, *this bird would be suspicious of an affectionate puppy.*

"It could," Jim conceded.

"Then why should I listen to you?"

"Because," Jim said, "when you accept our offer, old King Midas will look like a piker in comparison."

7.   A CAPSULE

As HE TALKED, with his cool persuasiveness, Jim watched the dictator's greedy eyes grow rapt. Jim pointed out that the rift between Aqaban's country and the West was too great for Aqaban to deal with the democracies. So far, Aqaban had had only one other choice: Zovoloff and his crowd. Jim needed hardly to remind Aqaban of the dangers and pitfalls along this road. Aqaban knew that treachery was normal and acceptable in Zovoloff's scheme of things. Once Zovoloff got what he was after, Aqaban's usefulness to him would end. Aqaban then might well face the status of a political slave, deposition from his place of power, or even assassination.

Aqaban's position had forced him to think of the Belorra formula as a political tool, a means of staying in power.

"But now you have another choice," Jim said. "We offer you the most powerful weapon of all, the economic. Why let the Belorra process leave Masacar at all? Why not keep it right here? Why not turn Masacar one day into a food funnel for the hungry nations of the earth? They'd have to come to you. A new balance of world power would be struck. The militarily strong nations would be at a stand-off, neither side daring to attack you. Excellency," Jim sighed, "all previous conquerors would be as children playing with wooden blocks."

Aqaban's hooded eyes tried to hide the glow in their depths. "You're prepared to finance the technical facilities, the research, the development, the building of factories and transportation?"

"For a generous slurp of the gravy." Jim nodded. He stood up and pushed back his chair. "That's our offer, in a nutshell. The details shouldn't be difficult. But, first, you must show us that we're not wasting time."

"Your organization is all-wise, Phelps," Aqaban said slyly. "You're supposed to know everything."

"We know you have a man. You say he is Dr. Hasman Belorra. You claim he has put a protein molecule together. Are you afraid to show me this man?"

"Of course not!"

"Then how about putting your dungeon cell where your luncheon table is?"

"Very well." Aqaban rose with the sinewy movements of a preying tiger. "But let me drop a word to the all-wise. If we get to the point of detailed discussion, you'd better match me proof for proof! Otherwise, you'd find the desert air of Masacar not at all healthy."

"Lead on," Jim said, with a short bow and sweeping invitation of his hand.

As he followed Aqaban's brisk steps, Phelps mapped the inside layout of the palace in his mind.

They rode a small elevator to ground level and stepped out on a portico that was shaded by a slanting roof supported on a long row of columns. Jim's glance swept across the lawn and adjacent garden. His toe stubbed. He almost missed a step. A gardener was trimming shrubs within a dozen paces of the sod trapdoor Willy and Barney had fashioned.

The gardener looked across at the portico. Seeing the bemedaled and gold-braided white uniform of the Big Man himself, the gardener speeded a final few snips and hurried toward a small hothouse where orchids grew. Jim let out a soft breath.

Aqaban had stopped at a steel-barred doorway where a guard was frantically tugging a massive iron bolt.

The guard snapped a salute as he pushed open the door. Aqaban favored him with a nod.

Aqaban paused just long enough to let Jim fall in step beside him.

"Strangely," Aqaban said with a small smile, "I rather like this part of the palace."

They moved down a narrow, short flight of stairs. The stones, like the damp-looking floor below, had been worn smooth by the shuffle of weary feet over a period of hundreds of years.

Partly underground, the corridor was lighted with glaring bulbs set in steel cages into the ceiling at intervals. But it felt dark to Jim. A slimy mildew corroded the walls and soon seemed to pervade Jim's clothing.

"Lots of activity down here in the old days." Aqaban smirked. "The caliphs knew how to rule. They didn't fool around."

Neither do you, Jim thought grimly. *Your enemies just don't seem to make it this far.*

Aqaban had stopped at a sheet-iron door that was blackened with brittle scales. He grasped the heavy bolt and slid it back. The door creaked on rusty hinges as he pulled it open.

The sounds of their approach had brought Dr. Belorra to stiff attention beside the lumpy, filthy cot. Jim's eyes widened. He drew in a short breath of amazement. The rugged durability, suggested by the photograph Jim had examined in Venice, had armed Dr. Belorra through his crushing ordeals. The chiseled, Grecian face was a little thinner. But the dark eyes were clear and undefeated. The husky shoulders retained their determined carriage. Even in the dirty, miserable prison cottons, Dr. Belorra remained an impressive figure.

As Aqaban mocked the doctor with a too-polite greeting, Jim glanced about the cell. What a rotten hole! His admiration for Belorra went up another notch when he noted the mathematical formulas with which the doctor had covered the mildewed walls. The man had used the cell itself to keep it from breaking him! *Bravo,* Jim thought.

Aqaban was strutting back and forth. "How'd you like a brand-new laboratory, Doctor? Fitted with all the latest gadgets?"

Belorra studied Jim, trying to fit him into the scheme of things.

"It's possible, Doctor." Jim nodded. "I represent a group which has just now entered the picture."

"He proposes that we Masacarians keep what we have," Aqaban said.

"We'd be in production months, even years sooner —with the originator of the process heading up the development program," Jim added.

"What do you say, Doctor?" Aqaban wheedled. "Phelps is suggesting that I offer you a way out. I'm willing to discuss restoration of your property—maybe even an official title."

"In your government?" Dr. Belorra asked calmly. "I think I prefer the cell. In here, at least, only my flesh will rot."

A vein pulsed in Aqaban's neck, but he held his voice at a calm level. "You can't have everything, Doctor. It's a generous offer. We'll give you a chance to think it over."

While Aqaban and Dr. Belorra locked stares, Jim moved his tongue inside his mouth. He slipped the tiny plastic capsule from its hiding place between his lower gums and jaw. The capsule had nestled there since early morning. At any moment during a search, he could have swallowed it.

"I don't need to think it over," Dr. Belorra said.

Jim raised his hand to his mouth. He coughed. The capsule fell into his palm.

Aqaban was giving the doctor a final glare. "We'll see about that! You may end up begging for a chance!"

With a quick jerk of his head, the dictator motioned Jim out. Hand hanging at his side, Jim let the capsule slide from his fingers. At the door, Jim paused. "Better take some good advice, Doctor. I suggest meticulous examination. You'll have to search hard to find hope—if you reject His Excellency's generous offer."

Dr. Belorra watched the door swing closed. He heard their departing footsteps. He eased to a sitting position on the edge of the cot. A deepening frown crimped his forehead.

Strangely, his first impression of this man Phelps had left him puzzled. Dr. Belorra's instincts for people were sharp, and the rangy, prematurely gray stranger somehow had seemed mismatched with Aqaban.

Dr. Belorra looked at the hateful door. His mind flashed an image of Phelps standing there. Was he imagining that Phelps had been trying to tell him something with his eyes in the final moment?

The peculiar words came back: meticulous examination . . . search hard. . . .

Search where?

The cell, of course. Where else?

Search for what? Hope, Phelps had said.

Was it possible? Dr. Belorra wondered if the dungeon was getting to him at last. *Am I going crazy—reading into words a meaning that went over Aqaban's head?*

His hands trembled slightly. He turned his head and looked about the cell. There was really nothing to search for in this barren hole. Meticulous examination wouldn't reveal a crack that he didn't know already. He knew them all so well—every speck of mildew, each tiny river the dampness made on the floor.

He suddenly stopped breathing. In slow motion, as if fearfully, he eased from the cot and crept a few feet toward the door.

The gleam that had caught his eyes was a small capsule. He quickly snatched it up. As he broke it apart and extracted a tiny coil of paper, he shifted into the light from the small, high window.

He unrolled the tissue and read: "You are not forgotten. Prepare yourself for forthcoming events. A girl will appear who is not your daughter. You must play it cool. Imagine that she really is Miriam, but that *you* are a ringer standing in for the real Dr. Belorra. You will understand everything fully in due time. Chew up and swallow message and capsule."

Dr. Belorra read the message twice. Then the words whirled together as a rush of tears filled his eyes.

During their return to the solarium, Aqaban tried to probe Jim with casual remarks about Dr. Belorra's condition and possibilities for the future. His side glances became more frequent as Jim's taciturn silence lengthened.

Closing the door on the heel-clicking solarium guards, Aqaban put it bluntly. "You're disturbed. Something is in your mind."

Jim studied the gardens through the glassed-in bay. "You first set eyes on Hasman Belorra when he was dragged before you. Right?"

Aqaban paused at the ivory table. It had been cleared in his absence. Icy carafes of tropical fruit drinks had been set out. "Does it matter?"

"It might. He had friends in Rome, colleagues, men of science. He visited there. It follows that his house here was open to them. How many came and went?"

Aqaban shrugged. "I've no way of knowing. The previous government wanted tourists and was stupidly lax with our frontiers. People moved freely, including"—his smile was waspish—"adventurers devoted to my cause."

"Exactly," Jim said bitterly.

Aqaban poured himself a glass of punch. While he poured, he cut short glances at Jim's broad back.

"My friend," he said, a chill edging into his voice, "this new mood that seems to have taken hold of you . . . I suggest you explain it."

Jim turned. He saw the temper in Aqaban's caliph-like eyes. Jim's brows lifted in surprise. Then his lips twisted in a wry laugh. "Was it that noticeable?"

"Indeed."

Jim scratched his jaw with his knuckles. "I'm not at

all sure that my own imagination isn't running away with me, but the man you have in the cell looks suspiciously like a physics professor in the university at Rome. He and Belorra bore a strong resemblance. If they knew each other, were friends. . . ." He shook his head, seeming impatient with himself. "But of course, it isn't possible! It would all have to dovetail too closely."

Aqaban stood with his drink forgotten.

"And yet. . . ." Jim paced from the window, eyes glazed with thought. "What if there were three people in Belorra's house the night the guards came? Belorra, Miriam, a visiting colleague? What if all three took flight and were separated. One, Miriam, did get away. We know that. But we don't know for sure that a second didn't."

Aqaban gripped his glass with crushing force. "Hogwash!"

"I hope so," Jim said amiably.

"But the game he plays! The markings on the cell walls that fill up his time!"

"Either Belorra—or a physicist—might have put them there," Jim said. He shook his head as if trying to cast out his doubts. "But his appearance, the way he has weathered interrogation and imprisonment, a man could take the ordeal that way if he knew a friend had escaped and was free to assist him in due time."

A vein swelled across Aqaban's forehead. "But I have the protein formula, safely hidden here in the palace!"

"You have *a* formula," Jim amended.

Aqaban's face burned purple with frustration. "First Zovoloff with his doubts, now you!" he burst out. Then he caught himself. His body shook with the effort to control himself.

Jim's lips pursed. "So Zovoloff raised the question of identity, also."

Aqaban slammed his glass onto the table, splattering the sleeve of his white uniform jacket with ruby red juice. "Not at all! He tried to sneak a preview of the formula with an impossible tale that men can cheat truth drugs."

"They can, as a matter of fact."

Aqaban thumped his chest. His face was oily with hot sweat. "But no one cheats Janar Aqaban! I'm the top man in this part of the world! I have Belorra. I have his formula. And I may choose not to do business with either you or Zovoloff!"

"Don't make rash boasts you may be sorry for," Jim suggested mildly. "We'll decide whether there is business to transact—when we have satisfied our own minds."

Jim strolled to the door and placed his hand on the gilded handle. He paused, looking over his shoulder. He favored the seething dictator with a friendly smile.

"I'm not underestimating your power in Masacar, Your Excellency. By your order, some very unpleasant things could happen to me. But I won't lose any sleep. You won't give the order—until you're certain I'm of no value to you."

Aqaban stood with his hands clenched at his sides. Each shallow breath was an effort. "I'm a generous host, Phelps." He forced the words out.

"Good. We figured you'd be." Jim's eyes were coaxing. "We can work together. It's just that you must give us time to make sure a certain physicist is still filling his chair at the university in Rome."

"All right. Settle your silly doubts, Phelps." Aqaban's words still came stiffly. "Meanwhile, confine your movements to the city."

"By all means." Jim depressed the handle and started to open the door.

Aqaban's voice caught him. "Phelps. . . ."

"Yes?"

Aqaban had returned to the table and was pouring himself a second glass. "I'm putting out special orders concerning unidentified helicopters."

"Understood." Jim's nod was amiable. "Your Excellency, I knew from the start that it would be impossible for me to get out the same way I got in."

With a flick of his hand Aqaban motioned Jim out of his presence. "A car will return you to the hotel."

"Your Excellency is most thoughtful."

Jim's nerves had just about ceased their tight singing when the car let him out in front of the Ibn Lhaso.

He dismissed the driver with a smile and stood there a moment on the sunny sidewalk. His mind backflashed over the meeting with Aqaban, detail by detail. Had he figured anything too closely, cut it too fine anywhere, made a slip that might turn into a noose about collective IMF necks?

He took a long breath and mounted the steps to the hotel lobby.

As he stepped inside, he jolted to a stop. From habit, his quick eyes had assessed the surroundings. The Nordic shape of the head of the stranger at the desk struck a note of caution.

Jim strolled to a chair at one side of the tall windows. He picked up a limp magazine from a table and sat down.

Opening the magazine and pretending to read, he watched the quiet conversation between the desk clerk and Captain Stefan Zovoloff. The distance across the lobby kept Jim from hearing the conversation.

But the meaning of Zovoloff's presence here was clear.

As had to be expected, Zovoloff had a spy inside the palace. He could be among the rank of men close to Aqaban, someone secretly coveting the boss man's job.

Word had been gotten to Zovoloff that a man named Phelps had been taken from the hotel to the palace. Zovoloff had naturally decided to ask a few discreet questions.

From the cover of the magazine, Jim watched Zovoloff turn at last from the clerk and stride from the lobby.

Our friend from the East has a worried and cautious look about him, Jim mused. He wished he could have the pleasure of watching when Zovoloff and Aqaban started fishing for each other in the dark.

8. MIRIAM AND LARA

THE DRIVE across the desert hadn't been too bad. Cinnamon Carter had purchased the secondhand Saab in El Khaba, the jumping-off place more than a hundred miles east of Masacar. The little sedan wasn't much for looks. The black paint was weathered to a lighter shade on the curve of fender and roof; the leather upholstery looked floppy and loose over seat springs that had sagged. But Cinnamon had given more attention to the zing in the engine, the tightness of steering and brakes.

The narrow road had run straight across the desert, a lumpy black ribbon that thinned to a needlepoint on the horizon. The land on either side had been vast and

empty, its flatness broken only by low dunes that gave
scant support to drab, brown vegetation.

Under the interminable fierceness of the sun, shim-
mering heat gave the road a constant look of wetness
far ahead of the humming car.

Traffic had been just about nonexistent. Now and
then they passed a big tractor-trailer truck going to or
from Masacar. The black spume from the big diesel
engines lingered in the dead air long after the rig
had swooped by.

But the ride had been far from boring or lonely.
There was, as always, the slight buildup of inner tension as the minutes ticked Cinnamon toward the job
ahead. Aside from that, Miriam Belorra had been
good company. She was intelligent, witty, companion-
able, buoyed by fresh hope for her father.

Cinnamon's slim fingers tightened on the steering
wheel as she saw the specks on the highway far ahead
in the heat haze. The little car ate up the torrid pavement yard by yard, and the specks took shape, be-
coming the dark, squarish shadows of trucks drawn
to a stop in a short line.

Cinnamon eased the Saab to a slower speed. She
drew in breath. "There's the border—the checkpoint. . . ."

Swiftly her mind devoted itself to a final review of
the part she was playing. The key to a successful
masquerade was to forget the disguise, to actually *be*
the other person.

From the moment they had left Rome, Miriam had
coached Cinnamon with details of her life that ex-

tended back into childhood. Miriam had been an excellent teacher, holding back nothing of her private feelings and thoughts. Cinnamon had soaked up everything. Even Miriam Belorra's little mannerisms quickly became hers.

In appearance, Cinnamon was the twin of the Miriam who had been in Rome. The transformation had been almost too easy for Rollin Hand's genius in the art of disguise.

Jim Phelps had chosen Cinnamon's dossier from the IMF file, Rollin had complained, because the two girls looked so much alike to start with that they could have been sisters.

"Why didn't you give me a challenge?" Rollin had grumbled good-naturedly. "Turning our own Cinnamon Carter into Miriam Belorra is child's play. Watch . . . a little shadowing here to elevate the cheekbones . . . tone down the highlights of the hair . . . a touch of wax inside the cheeks to round the chin . . . reshape the brows . . . the tiniest blackout on the edge of the eyetooth to shift the spacing . . . the contact lenses to shade the color of the eyes. . . ."

Rollin's quick hands had worked with his brushes, dyes, gum arabic, tweezers. Then he had stepped back and said with a grin, "Well, hi there, Miss Belorra— have a look at yourself!"

Cinnamon had pulled loose the towel with which Rollin had bibbed her. Straightening in her chair, she had accepted the hand mirror he offered.

"Rollin, you're a magician, no less."

"Please," he had complained, "save the flattery for

a time when it's more deserved."

Then he had turned to Miriam, who had stood staring at the image of herself.

"Now, you, dear girl," he'd suggested, "shall be a
quite nice teen-ager of Sicilian extraction. Your par-
ents work on the next estate down the road. You met
Miss Belorra when she was over there one day. You
have finished high school and wanted employment.
And so—a few minutes from now—you will become
Miss Miriam Belorra's personal maid."

Rollin had walked around the girl, studying her.
"Won't take much—dye the hair jet black . . . darken
the skin to a fine walnut gloss . . . make the lips a little
fuller and the lashes thicker . . . the eyes a very dark
brown. What shall your name be?"

"How about Lara?" Miriam had suggested.

"Excellent! A lovely name."

"It was my mother's," Miriam had said.

Cinnamon braked the Saab to a slow stop behind a
huge, dusty truck. The driver, a burly, swarthy man,
climbed from the cab. He stood in the shadow while
the inspection took place. A young border patrolman
in fawn-colored uniform questioned him and looked
at his papers. A second guard unbarred the heavy
tail gate and climbed inside to look over the cargo.

Cinnamon had time for a last look along the frontier. She had first seen those watchtowers from a distance. They rose like skinny black skeletons every few
miles until they were swallowed by the north and
south horizons. Cinnamon suspected they mounted
machine guns, and now that she was about to cross the

line they seemed much more personal.

Up ahead the driver was clambering into his cab. He took a minute to settle in his seat; then the engine started with a heavy growl. The rear of the van swayed a little on the uneven pavement as it trundled ahead. Gradually gaining speed, the truck was soon a diminishing shadow.

The guard who had questioned the truck driver stood to the left and motioned the Saab forward. A few yards behind him, the edge of Masacar was marked by a small station built of fresh-looking concrete and glass. It had the hulking sturdiness of a pillbox. A pair of high-powered machine guns showed their snouts through slits in the parapet roof.

Cinnamon stopped the small sedan as the guard commanded with a palm-up gesture.

He strode toward the driver's side, stalwart, with a nicely cut face. In the beginning he had probably idealized the revolution, Cinnamon thought to herself. The other guard looked more like a true Aqaban follower, coarse and cruel.

The first guard rested his hands on the car door. "Well! At last something much prettier than truck drivers!"

"I should hope so." Cinnamon laughed.

He opened the door. "Please hand the keys to the comrade for a look in the trunk, then step out."

Cinnamon handed the keys across Miriam to the hairy hand that was thrust in. She and Miriam slid from the seat.

"Your name, please," the young guard addressed

Miriam as she stepped out of the car.

"Lara, personal maid to my lady."

He smiled at Cinnamon. "And what are you called?"

"If you like, call me Miriam Belorra," Cinnamon said.

The trunk lid slammed. The guard charged around from the rear. "Cahsim! Did she say. . . ."

"She did." Cahsim's smile faltered.

The other guard grabbed Cinnamon's arm. "You may be worth a slight reward!"

Cahsim dropped his hand upon his companion's beefy shoulder. "Easy, Comrade. She's here of her own free will. I don't believe she'll run away." He stepped one pace aside. "Miss Belorra, you and Lara will go inside the station while I get in touch with my commanding officer."

Neatly modest in the walking shorts and tailored blouse she had chosen for driving, Cinnamon led the way into the border station. The outer office was clean but only sparsely furnished, with a desk, a few wooden chairs, and a filing cabinet.

Cahsim pointed at two chairs near the window.

"Please make yourselves as comfortable as possible." He disappeared through a doorway, while the other guard sat on the edge of the desk and watched the prisoners morosely.

Cinnamon and Miriam swapped a covert glance which said: *This is it . . . we're on our way*.

They could hear the muffled sound of Cahsim talking into a telephone. The conversation dragged for ten, twelve, fifteen minutes. Then the door across the room opened. He stood framed in it. "The Saab will have to be impounded. I'm to awaken one of the off-duty men. You'll be driven into Masarium."

"With an invitation to the palace?"

"Edged with iron, rather than gold, Miss Belorra." Cahsim's nod was bleak.

Cinnamon stood up. "Very well. But if I could ask one small favor."

"My rank doesn't entitle me to big promises, but ask away."

"It's quite small." Cinnamon glanced at the quiet submissiveness of Miriam. "Lara has no place to go, no one to depend on but me. She'd just be a bother to the people at the palace. I have money. Couldn't you arrange to register her at a hotel while I discuss business with His Excellency?"

"I don't see why not," Cahsim said. A brief smile tugged his mouth. "She doesn't look like an international Mata Hari. I'll do what I can."

"Thank you." Cinnamon snapped her hand in a salute so playful that it obviously covered deep concern. "Let's not keep the Big Man waiting."

Janar Aqaban agreed with those sentiments. Shuttered in his plush private office, he paced the thick carpet in restless excitement. Zovoloff's agents had missed Miriam Belorra in Rome. Instead, she was here—on her own initiative. The implications were more than interesting.

Aqaban strode behind his enormous white desk, flung himself into the soft leather chair, rocked back, and threw his feet on the desk.

First Phelps, Aqaban thought, and now the girl.

A frown tugged Aqaban's brows as his cunning mind picked at a no longer cut-and-dried situation. He regretted having jumped so quickly at the chance offered by Zovoloff and his crowd. But at the time Aqaban's political balance was uncertain. He'd had to have something tangible to calm the uncertainties of men whose support was crucial. He'd had to weld Masacar under the rule of a single iron hand, before the forces of opposition could organize.

Now that the situation had changed, Aqaban dreaded the prospect of going against Zovoloff. The foreign agent had the backing of massive power— if he chose to take off the gloves.

The lips in the hawkish face thinned. Aqaban's thoughts were like ferrets. He didn't want a complete break between Masacar and the Zovoloff bloc. At the same time, he didn't intend to give anyone the best of a bargain. He believed in letting others divide the shell, while he wormed the meat from the almond.

Aqaban renewed his courage with the thought that all of his life had been a daring gamble. And he had always won. He was warmed by an upsurge of belief in his destiny. He was an exception to the mass of mankind. Fate had plucked him out for a purpose. His star was in the heavens. And he would win again.

The soft hum of the communicator built into the desk jolted him. He swung his feet down, leaned forward, and flipped a button of the small console set flush in the corner of the desk.

"Yes?"

"Excellency." The voice was that of the captain of the elite palace guardsmen. "Everything checks out. Questions put to the girl. Identification by an ex-servant. Even a blouse that was among the things in her suitcase carries the label of a Masarium store. She was wearing it when she and her father took to their heels."

"Good!" Aqaban's lips writhed in a smile of moist glee. "Where is Miriam Belorra now?"

"In the palace, Excellency."

"Then quit wasting time!"

"By all means, Excellency."

Aqaban's fingertips drummed a nervous staccato on the desk top while he waited. Presently, Cinnamon was ushered in by a single guard. Aqaban jumped up and came around the desk. His face was a friendly mask.

"I hope the questions didn't annoy you too much, Miss Belorra."

"I had guessed I'd have a few to answer. The people who once knew me and my father don't give the palace as their address nowadays. I expected to be met by strangers."

Aqaban nodded a silent command for the guard to retire and stay on duty outside. Then the dictator touched Cinnamon's elbow, guiding her forward. "It's only a matter of routine," he said. "We can't have just everyone, claiming to be anybody, barging in, can we?"

Her anxious eyes searched his face. "How is my

father?" she asked in a strained voice.

"Quite well."

"In every way?" she pressed.

"Body, mind, and spirit," Aqaban said.

A sob filled her throat. A long-held tightness inside of her seemed to shatter. She swayed slightly. Aqaban took hold of her arm and helped her toward a large white leather chair. She crumpled and sat clutching the arms of the chair.

Aqaban bent forward for a closer look at her face. "Are you all right, Miss Belorra?"

"Oh, yes—I am now!" Her misty eyes took on a certain radiance. "When can I see him?"

"Any time you like."

She watched him return to the chair behind the desk. "I'm sorry I acted as I did just now, Mr. Aqaban. I've been half out of my mind with worry and fear."

Aqaban studied her from the loftiness of the desk.

"My own freedom was worse than chains," she said haltingly. "I felt I'd deserted my father. I couldn't stand it any longer. I had to come back."

"Even though you feared and hated me?"

"Love for my father was stronger than anything else I might have felt." She was silent a moment, staring at a spot somewhere beyond her toes. Then she lifted her head. "Hasn't there been enough of fear and hatred, Mr. Aqaban?"

"But I've never hated anyone, Miss Belorra! Everything I've done has been for the good of my country and its people." He rested his elbows on the desk. His sigh was heavy. "Sometimes I've had to move quickly.

The nation was in chaos. I couldn't always stop and explain everything that was in my mind and heart. As a consequence, I've been the victim of misunderstanding. You and your father might have avoided much distress if you'd given yourselves a chance to know me. I'm not an ogre."

"Have you told all this to my father, Mr. Aqaban?"

A wry smile flattened his lips. "Unfortunately your father—up to now—hasn't liked the sound of my voice. How could I reason with a man who wouldn't listen?"

"I came back to talk sense—to everyone, Mr. Aqaban."

"I'll be a better listener than your father has been," Aqaban said.

"The Aqaban government is an established fact," Cinnamon said. "It's a reality that my father and I both must accept."

"You can hardly wish me out of existence." Aqaban's laugh was heavy with smug self-satisfaction. "You've made a good start. Keep talking."

"You must admit a thing or two yourself, Mr. Aqaban."

His eyes reflected displeasure at being told what he must or must not do. But his voice was expansive. "I'm a broadminded man, Miss Belorra. Always open to suggestions."

"Then I suggest a compromise. If my father accepts the authority of your government, will you turn him loose?"

He thought about it, then nodded. "But not to leave Masacar. The world is too full of evil, greedy people who'd like to get their hands on his formula."

"Will you restore his home, his laboratory?"

The edge of the desk pressed Aqaban's flat-muscled midriff as he leaned forward. "Frankly, Miss Belorra, I'd like nothing better than to see your father take his rightful and honored place as the leading scientific citizen of the new Masacar! Who knows how many more discoveries lurk in that head of his?" He hesitated, his eyes veiling. "As a matter of fact, I'm toying with the idea of producing Belorra protein with factories set up right here in Masacar!"

Cinnamon's eyes snapped wide. "But that would take time and enormous capital."

"Your father's cooperation would save much of the time. And never mind about the capital." He grinned slyly. "I'm not without connections in international high finance."

Cinnamon was rigid in her chair, as if stunned. "You've opened up a whole new avenue of possibilities, Mr. Aqaban."

Aqaban rose and came around the desk. "Talk to your father, Miss Belorra. We can patch up our misunderstanding. Bring him around to my way of thinking—and he can write his own ticket."

He reached out, took her hand, and drew her to her feet. "In fact," he said with a wide smile, "your father should have the honor of cutting the ribbon when the first food factory is ready for production."

9. THE SCENE

DR. BELORRA sat on the edge of the hard cot and stared at the wall. The creeping mildew was slowly erasing the symbols and formulas. It didn't matter. He couldn't play the mental game any longer. The message in the tiny capsule had changed all that. All he could do now was wait, his mind scorched with questions.

He jerked his head as he heard the grating of the door bolt. He rose, tight-muscled, watching the scabrous portal creak open under the pressure of a hand outside.

Aqaban's resplendent white uniform, with its flamboyant gold braid and medals, materialized in the doorway. The dictator's gaze was sly. He had something up his fancy sleeve.

"You have a visitor, Doctor." Aqaban glanced over his shoulder into the corridor. "All right, my dear, you may come in."

Aqaban stepped aside, revealing the person behind him. Seeing the girl, Dr. Belorra thought for a moment he was going to faint. If he hadn't been warned in advance, he would have sworn the girl was Miriam. Even so, the shock of seeing her was paralyzing.

She hesitated, flicked a glance at Aqaban, then said in a husky voice, "Hello, Papa." She rushed across the cell and threw her arms about Dr. Belorra. The numbness snapped from his muscles. His arms jerked, puppet-like, as he returned the embrace.

His mind whirled, seared by the words of the capsuled message. *Play it cool . . . she is Miriam, but you are not Belorra . . . you are the pretender, not she. . . .*

Dr. Belorra didn't understand it all. It was strange, mixed up, even grotesque. But the girl had appeared, just as the message had promised. There were forces working to free him. He must obey blindly. No time for questions. No room for doubts. Or he would undo all that was being done for him.

"Miriam . . . I never expected . . . I can't believe you're here!"

She stepped back, looking at him from arm's length. "Papa"—she forced the word—"have they mistreated you?"

He glanced over her shoulder at Aqaban. "How did all this come about? Did your agents locate her and force her to come back?"

"Not at all. She returned voluntarily." The dictator thoughtfully plucked at his right earlobe as he studied them. "I must say, I expected something more in the reunion—an emotional outburst, tears of joy."

Cinnamon linked her arm with Dr. Belorra's. They sat down side by side on the cot.

He studied the face that was so much like Miriam's. "You shouldn't have risked coming here. Things would have worked out."

"I thought I was acting for the best."

"I know you did." Dr. Belorra slipped his arm about her shoulders, a belated fatherly gesture. "You mustn't fret, my child."

"I won't . . . Papa. Just as you say." She looked at Aqaban. He was leaning against the doorjamb with his arms folded, taking it all in with narrowed eyes.

"Can't I have a few minutes alone with my father?" Cinnamon asked.

"To pass a few secrets?" Aqaban glared suspiciously. "Request denied."

"But I only. . . ."

"Anything not fit for my ears shouldn't be said at all." Aqaban peeled himself from the doorjamb and snapped his fingers. "Let's get down to business."

Dr. Belorra cast a quick, questioning glance at Cinnamon.

"He will free you . . . Papa," she said.

"On what condition?"

"That I get a little cooperation," Aqaban said. He edged toward them with catlike steps. His glance shuttled between them. "You do have the means to cooperate?"

"If you're referring to my knowledge of protein, of course I have the means." Dr. Belorra glowered. "But perhaps not the will."

"Papa. . . ." Cinnamon touched his arm.

"Don't wheedle, child!" Dr. Belorra jerked away. "This fellow has already had my cooperation—with his questions."

"Now I'm prepared to make a trade—if you can deliver," Aqaban said. "Why not build the food factories right here in Masacar, with Dr. Hasman Belorra at their head?"

"I can think of several million reasons," Dr. Belorra said. "Money. Money for the tools of development, laboratories, research assistants. Money for buildings and expensive specialized equipment. Money to train personnel. Money for a transportation system." Dr. Belorra snorted. "Is Masacar suddenly an industrial power like the United States?" After a moment he added, "Oh . . . Mr. Phelp's group. . . ."

"Forget about that. Leave it to me," Aqaban said. "Just think how nice it would be to have everything restored, in full measure and running over."

A mingling of caution and bewilderment crept into Dr. Belorra's face. He dropped his eyes from Aqaban's. "I'll have to think it over," he mumbled.

"That would be the intelligent thing to do—and under the circumstances I'm sure you will make the correct decision," Aqaban said. With a quick gesture he indicated to Cinnamon that the visit was over.

She got up, then bent to touch Dr. Belorra's forehead with a brief, good-bye kiss. "You're not to worry anymore, Papa."

He looked into Miriam's face, into the friendly, encouraging eyes of a stranger. "I won't. And thank you for coming."

The eyes moved in a secret nod; then she turned and passed by Aqaban.

"Miriam. . . ." The name came slowly from Dr. Belorra's lips.

Cinnamon stopped and looked back from the corridor. "Yes, Papa?"

"Where is. . . ." He bit the question back in time. A sheen of nervous sweat was suddenly on his forehead. "Nothing . . . forget it," he said. "I . . . we can talk later . . . all of us."

With a final sharp glance at Dr. Belorra, Aqaban stepped into the corridor and pulled the heavy door. The bar ground into its socket.

Body strained rigidly, Dr. Belorra listened to their footsteps go away. He bit his lips to keep from shouting the question after them: Where is the real Miriam? What has happened to my daughter?

Cinnamon steadied her breathing as she walked with Aqaban to his office. She hoped her nervousness wasn't showing. In the last moment Dr. Belorra had almost blurted out the ruin of everything. Cinnamon understood his need to know about Miriam. She had a small ache inside herself; she was suffering with him. She fervently wished she could reassure him with the truth.

But what was the truth? The truth was that everybody was still deep in the woods and the hunters were dangerous. The truth included the hope that Dr. Belorra did not crack under the strain.

The truth was the present glittering threat in Aqaban's eyes, steel pinpoints, as he faced her from behind his ornate desk.

"Miss Belorra, who is the man in the cell?"

She sat down slowly, her eyes, showing puzzlement, on his face. "Whatever do you mean?"

"Just what I say! Is that man Dr. Hasman Belorra, your father?"

"That man," she said distinctly, "is Dr. Hasman Belorra."

Her open honesty was obviously too much for his devious mind to accept at face value.

"What are you driving at, Mr. Aqaban?"

"I saw your shock of surprise, your hesitation. Oh, yes, I saw all the little signs. I'm not exactly a fool, you know. You tried, Miss Miriam Belorra, but you didn't play the scene very well!"

Cinnamon stared with wide, bewildered eyes. "Scene, Mr. Aqaban?"

"There in the cell!" he snarled. "You know what I'm talking about. The father-daughter reunion was as phony as anything I've ever seen. You knew the wrong man was in the cell the minute I opened the door."

"I don't know what else I can say," she said helplessly. "On my honor, Mr. Aqaban, the man down there is Dr. Hasman Belorra."

"I think you insist a little too much, Miss Belorra!"

He picked up a golden letter opener and pressed the tip against the desk top. "What's the name of the physicist?" he asked cunningly. "The one at the university in Rome? You and your father know him quite well."

"Do you mean that you suspect— Oh, no! You're mistaken, Mr. Aqaban."

"But, no! A man named Phelps said . . . but never mind. The way things are stacking up, I trust Phelps more than I do you!"

"Why would I lie?"

Unconsciously, Aqaban was marring the desk with short jabs of the letter opener. "If the man in the cell isn't your father, you'd stall a new manhunt as long as you could."

"What else can I say?" Cinnamon spread her hands. Light caught briefly on the ring she wore on the little finger of her left hand. "If your prisoner isn't Dr. Hasman Belorra in the flesh, wouldn't I have known? If my father had escaped from Masacar, wouldn't he have gotten in touch with me? Why would I have risked coming here?"

Aqaban's saturnine face was a study in dark confusion. Then he threw the opener onto the desk. Striding to the side of the office, he barked a command, "Come here, Miss Belorra."

Cinnamon obediently hurried to his side. As he studied the innocence of her face with his squinty-eyed stare, Cinnamon worried her hands nervously together.

Aqaban turned to the wall niche beside him. In it

reposed a small marble bust of some all-but-forgotten minor official.

While Aqaban's back was to her, Cinnamon pressed her ring with her thumb. The setting—it appeared to be a small, black, semiprecious stone—dropped unseen into her right palm.

Aqaban had lifted out the small statue. Its beveled base was a cover for a secret compartment. Cinnamon's eyes showed a flicker of appreciation. The hiding place was excellent. Such niches were common in the palace. There were two in each side wall of the office, each a sanctuary for its statuette of marble or bronze. The simplicity of the miniature secret vault was a stroke of genius. A squad of trained men might have covered every inch of the office and come up emptyhanded.

Aqaban's hand disappeared. He lifted out a folded oblong of stiff white paper. It crackled as he spread it and thrust it at Cinnamon's face.

"What is this, Miss Belorra?"

Her response was automatic. Casually she took the parchment-like sheet and studied it a moment. She glanced over its edge.

"It's a formula, of course. But don't ask me to interpret it."

"You were your father's assistant," he said.

Cinnamon nodded. "I helped a great deal. Transcribed notes. I can operate a centrifuge and run a titration. I was great at the simple lab routine. But the higher aspects of his calculations and experiments were a bit beyond me."

Aqaban's lips twisted in angry impatience. "Would you care to hazard a guess?" he asked scathingly.

"Why not?" Cinnamon studied the formula and biochemical diagrams with which a neat, precise, experienced hand had covered the page. "It looks as if my father has given you directions for a synthetic protein molecule. Isn't that what you were after?"

Cinnamon refolded the paper. The black setting from her ring felt as if it were stuck to her damp palm. She had the fleeting fear that she wouldn't get rid of the setting at the only split-second opportunity.

She gave the formula a waggle under Aqaban's nose. "Mr. Aqaban, I do recognize the handwriting—which I'm sure you were going to ask about next. No one but the genuine Dr. Belorra made those little hummingbird tracks."

While she talked, Cinnamon offhandedly extended her arm and dropped the formula back into its secret receptacle. Unseen, the black ring setting went with it. The surface of the phony stone was a thin shell for a minute electronic energy cell. Cinnamon imagined she heard it strike like a soft raindrop.

Aqaban was still trying to read behind her eyes. She knew his difficulty. So much had been thrown at him that he needed time to sort out the conflicting elements. His wasn't the kind of mind that cuts straight through to the heart of a problem. He always had to take a sneaky roundabout. And thank goodness for that!

He replaced the statue, giving it a jiggle to make sure it was seated.

Cinnamon controlled the urge to whoop out a relieved burst of breath. In her mind's eye she imagined the energy cell nesting under the formula, pulsing a tiny heartbeat.

Aqaban tramped behind his desk. "Very well, Miss Belorra. I'll give you one last chance to change any of your statements."

Cinnamon's eyes were cool. "I suspect you're one of those men who won't be satisfied with anything short of a yes-man answer. What do you want to hear?"

"Don't get flip with me, young lady!" Aqaban hit the desk with a karate chop. "There are ways of making sure who the prisoner is."

"I've told you that."

"Then we'll think about amnesty for your father— if you can talk some sense into him. But if you're sticking to a foolish lie...."

"I quite understand, Mr. Aqaban. I'm not afraid of the outcome."

"I'll send you under escort to the Hotel Ibn Lhaso," Aqaban said. "You will check in there. You and your maid will have reasonable freedom of movement until I get to the bottom of things."

Cinnamon taunted him with a faint grin. "I understand. I'm a guest, but on a short rope in case you decide to lower the boom."

Aqaban's teeth glinted wolfishly. "You'd insult my hospitality if you tried to leave Masacar, Miss Belorra."

Cinnamon watched him press a button on the desk console to summon a guard. "My father taught me better manners than that, Mr. Aqaban."

Miriam Belorra had a pins-and-needles look about her when Cinnamon walked into the hotel room. But Miriam masked her agitation as she waited for a young guard to set a pair of suitcases inside the doorway.

"Lara," Cinnamon said, "you may unpack a few things. His Excellency released the bit of luggage we brought along."

"Yes, Miss Belorra," Miriam said.

Then, when the door had closed behind the guard, Miriam rushed to Cinnamon. Cinnamon touched the girl's trembling lips with a warning forefinger. She took the slender icy hand and led Miriam to the windows, as far from the door as possible.

"Yes," Cinnamon whispered, "Phelps, with that uncanny knowledge of people, place, and circumstance, called the shots. I did get to see your father, and he is well."

Miriam started to speak. Instead, her eyes flooded. She choked a note of gratitude.

Cinnamon's nod expressed compassion and understanding. "I know. You feel like a good healthy cry. So go ahead."

A breath shuddered into Miriam's lungs. She knuckled a tear from the corner of her eyes. "No," she said huskily. "I can save it for a more convenient time. Are they feeding him well? Is he thin? Have they . . . hurt his spirit . . . tortured him?"

"In a word," Cinnamon said with a smile, "he's come through tough. You've a real man for a father."

Miriam glanced into Cinnamon's eyes and was instantly satisfied that Cinnamon was holding nothing back.

"How about that unpacking?" Miriam suggested brightly.

"Sure. Might as well get acquainted with our accommodations."

"Pretty groovy, as Americans say," Miriam said. "I took a tour after His Unexcellency phoned the hotel, while you were on your way. Two bedrooms and this little sitting room."

"Fine," Cinnamon said. "We don't want to see too much of it. Get them used to our strolling out, reading in the park, poking among the shops."

"I understand," Miriam said. "Naturalness—that's the word. Just two young girls who don't like to stay indoors."

"Check." Cinnamon picked up one of the bags beside the door and headed into an adjoining bedroom.

She was closing a bureau drawer when she heard the imperious rapping of hard knuckles on the sitting room door. She started, then checked herself. It was a maid's job to answer the door.

She heard Miriam's movement across the sitting room from the bedroom on the other side. The door latch clicked.

"Yes?" Miriam said.

"I'm looking for Miss Miriam Belorra." The man speaking from the hallway had a chill voice that clipped words precisely.

"I'm Lara, the maid," Miriam said. "Who is calling?"

"Captain Stefan Zovoloff."

A quick pinch went through Cinnamon's shoulders as she listened.

"Please give me a moment, Captain," Miriam was saying. "I'll see if Miss Belorra is in."

"It's all right, Lara," Cinnamon said, strolling into the sitting room. "You can finish unpacking."

"Yes, ma'am." Miriam's movement suggested a curtsy. She turned and hurried into the bedroom.

"You wished to see me?" Cinnamon decided that this muscular Nordic was every bit as hard as he appeared in his photograph.

His manner right now was stiffly correct. "I'm sorry I missed your visit to the palace, Miss Belorra."

Her brows arched. "You were told about that?"

"I'm a temporary resident of the palace myself." He smiled. "I like to keep tabs on what is going on. I'm always interested in my surroundings, wherever I may be staying."

"Really?" She stepped aside. "Please sit down. I'm sorry I can't offer you refreshment. We are just now checking in."

She sank into an upholstered chair facing the one he chose. "You're not a Masacarian, Captain Zovoloff."

"Hardly."

"Are you a member of a trade mission?"

"You might say that," Zovoloff said. His hands rested idly on his knees. He studied his blunt fingertips. "Were you able to see your father?"

She waited a moment to speak. "I thought you knew everything that went on."

"I can't be every place at once." His smile didn't hold humor. "I know you came to the palace. I heard that you were Miriam Belorra. I learned that you had been assigned quarters here in the Ibn Lhaso. I assumed you returned to Masacar to see your father. I had the friendly hope that you had succeeded."

Her shoulders rose and fell with her sigh. "I certainly need all the friendly hopes I can get."

"You have mine in abundance. So does your father."

"Thank you, Captain."

He was studying her closely, framing words, when a breezy knock preceded the opening of the door.

Jim Phelps stood there a moment, his hand frozen on the knob. "Sorry, Miss Belorra. Didn't know you had company."

"I didn't expect any." Cinnamon laughed to recover her composure.

"I'll drop back by. . . ."

"Not at all," Zovoloff interrupted. He had paled a shade. His jaw muscles rippled. His eyes were cold. He tried to control his voice. "I was just leaving."

Cinnamon walked Zovoloff to the door. "Thanks for dropping in, Captain—and for the good hopes."

His eyes flicked in Jim's direction, then came back to her. "All of us need them at times. Good day, Miss Belorra."

"Anytime, Captain."

Zovoloff's heels clicked. He gave them both a nod, turned, and strode briskly down the hallway.

Cinnamon eased the door closed and fell back against it. Neither she nor Jim spoke until the sound of Zovoloff's tread diminished to nothing.

"Confound it," Jim exploded softly. "I wanted him to link us up, but not so quickly."

Cinnamon came across the room. Miriam slipped out of the bedroom. The three stood in a tight group, looking at the hallway door.

"He's more suspicious of Aqaban than ever," Miriam said. "From in there, I saw his face."

"He's trying to add up figures scattered in the wrong columns," Cinnamon said. "It won't dovetail to his satisfaction. He starts off with a natural suspicion of Aqaban, Aqaban of him. It's the way of con men. Then Jim appears from nowhere. Next, me. Finally, Zovoloff finds that Jim and I aren't strangers. It'll give the captain plenty of food for thought—the indigestible kind. He and Aqaban will both play it a lot sneakier from here on out."

"As if they weren't sneaky enough to start with," Miriam said. "Isn't this what we wanted?"

"But not like a handful of grit in our timing," Phelps said. "I wanted Cinnamon's report—and I didn't expect our boy so quickly." He walked to the windows and eased the curtain back. He saw Zovoloff leave the hotel and cross the sidewalk below. The captain got in the rear seat of a heavy black car. The driver swished it from the curbing.

Jim let the curtain fall. He rubbed the hardness of his jaw with his knuckles. "Keep your fingers crossed. If the captain feels a real bind, I've a hunch he'll run true to form. His daggers will start shedding scabbards all over the place."

10.   TWO ESCAPES

IN THE DESERT NIGHT the vandalized house, where Dr. Belorra and Miriam had once lived, was a pile of gloomy shadows. The walls of the fire-damaged west wing tottered like black, jagged teeth against the backdrop of purple, moon-hazed sky. The broken windows stared like empty eyes. The silence was suggestive of bottomless pits. The repellent air of desertion and decay was a reminder of the violence and disaster that had struck here with a fury only slightly less than that of a desert windstorm. It was little wonder that the natives gave the spooky place a wide berth.

In a small room in the east wing, Rollin Hand was

busy with his pet occupation. He was creating a disguise. With the window opening blacked out by a curtaining blanket, the interior of the barren cubicle was lighted by a small but powerful electric torch.

In the glow Rollin sat cross-legged, yoga-style, on the floor. Facing him was the small case he had opened. His reflection stared back from the mirror in the upraised lid.

Across the room Willy Armitage and Barney Collier sat on the hard floor, backs resting against the wall. They were quiet as they watched Rollin work.

Already his appearance was altered. The line of chin and jaw had shifted. The forehead looked a bit higher.

Rollin turned his head slightly, studying himself in the mirror. His hand dipped into the case. He lifted out a wisp of hair, touched his brows, and the brows ceased to belong to Rollin Hand.

He shifted the torch a few inches and instead of looking at his reflected image, his eyes picked at details of the large, glossy photograph of Dr. Hasman Belorra which was propped against the front of the case.

Rollin muttered some directions to himself, then touched a thin black grease pencil to the corners of his eyes. Tiny crow's-feet appeared. A wrinkle creased the forehead.

With deft, professional speed, his hands moved between the case and his face. The ears flattened. The nose hooked slightly. Near the left corner of the mouth a tiny mole appeared.

Then the man who had ceased to be Rollin Hand nodded. The mirrored image of Dr. Hasman Belorra dutifully nodded back.

Rollin dropped the photograph in the case, lowered the lid, and snapped the latch. He stood up and dusted off the seat of his trousers. He hoped the coarse brown cotton garments were close enough to Masacarian prison issue.

Neither Willy or Barney remarked on the almost magical disguise. It was their way of ribbing him, Rollin knew.

"Thanks for the compliment, fellows," Rollin said. "I see that my artistry has left you speechless."

"Okay," Willy growled. "So the job is great—Dr. Belorra."

"I wonder how well he crawls through two thousand-year-old aqueducts." Barney grinned.

"It sounds like my bag," Rollin said. "Let's go!"

Forty minutes later they were three humped shadows blending with the low piles of dirt at the archaeological diggings.

In the distance the lighted minarets of the palace stood like unreal spangles against the night sky.

Their eyes probed the heavy shadows of trenches and terraces. They saw the moving shadow almost at the same time. The man was about two hundred yards away, hurrying in the direction of the city. They watched until the darkness had swallowed him.

"The overseer," Barney whispered, "with his inside track. No change in security regulations—or he wouldn't be out here to pick up his bit of stashed bric-a-brac."

"It means," Willy added, "that now there's nobody here but us kittens."

Barney led the way. They eeled silently along terraces, across trenches, over ridges of loose, soft earth.

Long minutes later Barney's shadow disappeared over a dark edge. Rollin crawled in his wake, down the slope, into the bottom of a trench. A tiny landslide of earthen crumbs preceded Willy's arrival.

They paused to rest briefly in the black crevice.

"Almost there," Barney whispered. "Easy does it as we clear the rubble from the mouth of our molehole."

They crept forward. Rollin bumped into Barney's halted shadow.

"Over here," Barney said softly, giving Rollin a touch.

Hunkered on their knees, Rollin and Barney pushed aside a layer of loose dirt. Rollin's nails struck stone.

"I'll get that," Willy said. His figure bent beside Rollin. He grunted softly as his fingers dug under the edges of the thin stone slab. He lifted carefully and eased the covering to one side. A dark, roughly circular emptiness was exposed, just about the size of a manhole in a city street.

"Just don't snag and hang the seat of your pants going in. It's roomier inside," Barney promised.

"But not much," Willy added. "Watch you don't crack your head."

Barney went into the aqueduct headfirst, the dark hole swallowing him slowly.

Rollin counted off ten seconds for Barney to get ahead and clear, then he followed. The air was stale, suggesting something mummified. The stone felt like sandpaper against Rollin's knees and palms as he achieved the fast pace that Barney was setting. Behind him, he heard the muffled thuds of Willy's elephantine movements.

With the entrance a safe distance behind, Barney turned on a small pen-cell light. Sometime later the illumination showed an apparent blockage of the tunnel ahead, stone and dirt that Willy and Barney had torn from the roof.

Barney wriggled around to a sitting position and played the light upward. Rollin crowded beside him, craning his neck. He could see the small roots with their tiny clumps of clinging dirt, the glint of the triangular metal brace that kept the sod trapdoor from collapsing.

"Got it pictured in your mind?" Barney asked.

Rollin withdrew his head, nodding.

Barney turned off the light and Rollin heard the rustling movements, the slight spillage of dirt, as Barney wedged himself upward.

The faintest light filtered down as Barney lifted the trapdoor. Rollin's hand groped in the space where Barney's knees and calves had been. His finger met emptiness. Barney had pulled himself out into the palace grounds.

Rollin felt his heartbeat as he twisted about and struggled toward an upright position. Overhead, the exit was a blob of gray in the darkness. As Rollin's head and shoulders emerged, Barney grabbed him by the hand and gave him a lift. Squirming clear, Rollin dropped to one side behind the screening stand of shrubbery.

Through breaks in the foliage, Rollin quickly took stock. A short distance away he saw a portion of the palace—arched windows, a long, shadowy portico with columns. Much of the interior of the palace appeared to be brightly lighted behind silken draperies.

Suddenly he heard a murmured laugh. His hand shot into the hole to give a warning touch to the top of Willy's rising head.

Barney had also heard the nearby sound. Both he and Rollin froze, a clamp on their breathing.

With straining eyes Rollin glimpsed the source of the sound. Two guards had come out and were walking along the portico. Because of the shrubbery they were in and out of Rollin's line of sight. He began to breathe again. They were merely going from one part of the palace to another, laughing over a joke of their own.

The sound of a door closing behind them came across the side lawn. Rollin waited a few moments longer, then lifted the signaling pressure of his hand from Willy's head. Willy's face appeared out of the hole like a full moon with blinking eyes. Rollin and Barney each took an armpit and gave Willy an assist.

They moved out in single file with Barney in the lead.

Bodies crouched, they worked their way along the

wall, using the lush greenery of the tropical garden
as a cover.

Reaching the limits of the stand of shrubbery, they
paused. The grounds lay serene and softly shadowed.
Barney signaled with a quick nod. He was visible for
an instant, a tall, lean blue shadow in native costume,
as he covered the stretch of lawn on feet as silent as
a jaguar's pads. Then he disappeared from sight in the
dense shadow cast by the corner of the palace.

Rollin was next, a quick, flitting mirage in the night.
He dropped to his knees and crouched beside Barney.
Almost before Rollin had a chance to draw breath,
Willy was beside them.

They inched around the corner, the palace rearing
over them. This section of the building was dark; it
seemed to be gripped in a deathlike stillness. From
some other part of the huge building stereo music
drifted over the lawns and gardens.

"Okay," Barney whispered. "Got it!"

Willy and Rollin pressed against the stone while
Barney bellied flat on the ground and pulled himself
a few more inches.

Barney gripped the steel bars of the ground-level
window and pressed his face between two of them.

"Dr. Belorra!" he hissed. "We're friends. Come to
take you out."

From the cell came a startled gasp of sound.

"Quiet!" Barney's whisper stung. "You want the
palace down around our ears?"

The cot rustled as Dr. Belorra stepped upon it. His
face was a pale blur suddenly swimming in the dark-

ness on a level with Barney's.

"Who are you?" Dr. Belorra whispered. "My daughter . . . is she. . . ."

"She's fine. No more questions now. You'll learn everything later."

"All right. How are you going to get me out of here? What are your instructions?"

"I'll slice out two of the bars with a small hand laser," Barney said. "Make sure you stand clear. I'll give you five seconds."

The creak of the cot told them that Dr. Belorra had moved away.

Willy unwound a foot-wide band he had worn about his waist. He and Rollin stretched it between them. As they unfolded it, it became a bed-size sheet of black plastic.

Rollin took one corner, Willy the opposite. With a single motion they pressed the edge of the plastic against the wall, letting it fall across Barney.

Even through the black material the flare of the tiny laser was dimly visible. The high energy beam, no larger around than a needle, sliced through the bars like a knife through mud. The acrid smell of seared metal filtered from under the black camouflage.

"Okay," Barney said softly.

Rollin and Willy whipped away the plastic, reduced its size with a few quick folds, and Willy stuffed it under his jerkin.

Rollin dropped beside Barney and tossed the small laser case to Willy. It promptly disappeared, nestling with the plastic.

Two of the bars emitted a hairline glow across each end.

"They're all yours, Willy," Barney whispered, inching to one side.

Willy's hand dipped through a slit in his pantaloons, dug in a baggy pocket, and came out holding a small asbestos pad.

Without hesitation, he lifted out the bars, using the pad to shield his fingers. He laid them side by side, close to the smooth stone of the wall.

"Dr. Belorra?" Barney whispered.

"Here."

"We're ready. Welcome to a breath of fresh, free air!"

They heard Dr. Belorra step onto the cot. His hands snaked through the opening in the narrow window and gripped the sharp edge of stone. Rollin and Barney stood to each side. As Dr. Belorra's head and shoulders wriggled through, they grabbed hold of the waistband of his trousers and helped him out.

He lay full length on the grass for a moment, his face and body drinking in the sweetness of it. As he pulled to his feet and fell back against the wall, unashamed tears glinted on the gray shadow of his face.

"Bless you, whoever you are." His whisper was choked.

Barney had time only to acknowledge the thanks with a nod. Rollin Hand had already turned. Crawling backward, he had dropped his feet inside the cell.

Seeing the movement, Dr. Belorra realized what was happening. He dropped beside Barney, who was holding Rollin's arm as Rollin slid farther inside.

"No, no!" Dr. Belorra said, his voice almost rising above a whisper. "I can't buy my own freedom that way—not with another man taking my place. Besides, the minute they see him. . . ."

"He looks enough like you to be a twin, Doctor," Barney said. "If the lighting was better, you'd see for yourself."

"But I can't permit. . . ."

"Keep your voice down! And be assured we've a plan to take our man out when the time comes—if fortune smiles and the gears all mesh. In case of a snafu, it won't matter whether he's in there or running with the rest of us through the wilds of Masacar."

Rollin had disappeared inside. Dr. Belorra murmured, "My friend—whose name I don't even know—good luck."

Willy picked up the two bars and set them back in place. His hands made quick motion at their ends.

"I can't see to make out exactly what he's doing," Dr. Belorra said against Barney's ear.

"Wrapping the cuts in the bars with a thin plastic tape, the color of iron. The bars will pass a quick inspection—unless somebody steps up for a closer look."

"What am I to do now?" Dr. Belorra asked. "There is still the wall around the grounds with a guard at every entry."

"But one," Barney amended. "It's our private subway. This man is called Willy. Go with him. He will show you."

"And you, my young friend?"

"Still got a little hanky-panky inside the palace that should prove interesting," Barney said.

Willy touched the doctor's shoulder. "We'd better get a move on, sir."

Dr. Belorra's hand fumbled and found Barney's in the darkness. The clasp was quick, firm. Then Barney watched Willy's and Dr. Belorra's shadows dash across the lawn. They melted behind the shrubbery.

Motionless, Barney timed their movements, holding himself as a force in reserve if they ran into trouble.

Nothing broke the serenity. Willy and Dr. Belorra should be well into the aqueduct now, the sod trapdoor back in place.

Barney lowered his face to the window. "So long, Doc."

"You still here?" Rollin's disembodied whisper floated from the cell.

"On my way. Just another servant in the palace." Barney crept away from the window and circled the lawn to the shadows of a rose arbor. The trellis arched over a flagstone walkway. When he emerged, Barney's furtiveness had vanished. He strolled across the flagstones with the casual ease of a man who had traveled the route a thousand times.

His palms dampened and a tightness pulled through his throat as he boldly entered the palace through a rear door.

Ahead was a stone corridor. It was barren, lighted by unshaded bulbs, and studded here and there with unadorned wooden doors. None of the artistry that lent such grace to the rest of the palace had been wasted on the servants' quarters. A slim servant girl came from a doorway just ahead. She accepted Barney's presence with hardly a glance as she hurried to some task on quick, sandaled feet.

The farther end of the corridor was an arched opening onto a small courtyard. Barney's stride toward it was purposeful, as if he were moving under orders from Aqaban himself.

Crossing the narrow court, Barney slipped the transistorized receiver from the waistband of his pantaloons and hid it in his palm. It was about the size of a silver dollar. He curled his middle finger and depressed the button, activating the electronic detector.

Briskly he opened a brass-studded door and entered the wing of the palace without hesitation. He was in a short hallway that opened into a small indoor garden under a high glass dome. He chose a corridor at random, the one to his right. He lifted his hand, the gesture of a man pressing a palm against an aching ear. The whispered blips emitted by the receiver faded. Barney gritted his teeth, turned, and retraced his steps.

This time when he entered the indoor garden, a burly guard in fawn uniform was passing through. Barney gave him a respectful nod with downcast eyes. The guard didn't bother to return the polite salutation.

The blips grew stronger as Barney hurried along a corridor with thick carpeting and polished marble wainscoting.

Now and then the echoes of life in the palace drifted to him—muted music, an extraordinarily loud guffaw.

The detector in Barney's sweating palm increased its activity. It became an angry bee, buzzing Morse code dots.

Barney's blood quickened. The pulsator, which Cinnamon had planted with the Belorra formula, couldn't be more than a few yards away.

He reached an ell and knew at once that his destination must lie beyond the tall, double doors just ahead. But his stomach shriveled. Standing duty at the doorway was a young guard. He looked alert and capable.

Barney didn't let the development discourage him. Without breaking stride, he moved toward the guard.

"Who are you?" he demanded.

The guard frowned at being so accosted by a servant in menial clothing.

"I'm Rabba," he said icily. "But of what concern is that to you?"

"Nothing to me," Barney said with just the right amount of sneer. "But plenty to you. His Excellency wants to see you—now. Immediately."

The guard frowned. "What about?"

Barney lifted and dropped his shoulders. Then he lowered his voice to a confidential tone. "Don't quote me, but the captain of the guard may have been talking with His Excellency about you."

The young face went parchment pale.

"You'd better hurry, if you like your skin whole," Barney suggested.

The guard hesitated. "I can't leave this post without direct orders." His eyes narrowed. "Who are you? I haven't seen you around the palace before."

Barney felt as if something were about to snap inside of him. He had a single final second before the guard became really suspicious.

"I've been around for. . . ." He was casually gesturing with his empty palm as he started to speak. Then the motion was anything but casual. The movement was so lightning quick that the guard hardly saw the karate chop.

The blow was not intended to seriously injure, in keeping with the IMF code. Phelps had once summed it up in a single statement: "Cruelty traded for cruelty leaves the world right where it was, or worse, so let the viciousness of the cruel be their own undoing."

The guard slumped, temporarily stunned. Barney caught him under the armpits. He eased the guard to the carpet, turned, and tried the gilded door handles which were shaped like nightingale's wings.

The latches resisted the pressure of his hands. He dropped to one knee beside the guard. Beads of sweat were squeezing from Barney's face. His ears strained for the sound of a footfall.

He lifted a pair of keys from the guard's tunic, sprang to the door, and inserted one. It turned. He shoved the doors open, grabbed the guard by the shoulders, and dragged him inside.

Closing the door with a soft click, Barney looked over his surroundings, a soft whistle threading through his teeth. Could anyone really get down to work in an office like this? Barney wondered. Two-story vaulted ceiling. Polished mosaics and niches with rare bits of statuary relieving the sweeping expanses of walls. The whole dominated by the desk at the farther end of the long room. Ivory, no less. A desk so huge it might have served a travel bureau in Grand Central Station.

Barney held his detector at shoulder height as he padded deeper into the room. The activity against his palm became a tingling, impelling buzz.

It slackened, and he turned back from a point near the desk. The intensity of the blips again increased. The invisible beam drew him to a stop in front of a wall niche. He stood frowning. His fingers explored the wall about the niche. He took a breath, knuckled sweat from his forehead, and tried the inside, feeling for a crack, a section of masonry that would move.

No luck. He shook his head and swallowed dryness from his throat. Whoever had designed the hiding place had certainly concealed its triggering device well.

Then his eyes fastened on the small statue resting so innocently inside the niche. He grabbed it and pushed. The bust emitted a faint sound of stone grating against stone.

But it wasn't a lever that would open a section of wall. It didn't respond to Barney's shoving or tugging, except to feel slightly loose and give out a gritty sound. But when he lifted the bust, it rose freely, its thick, beveled base parting from the matching, surrounding stone. He shook his head.

"Well, who would have thunk?" Barney muttered. His free hand disappeared in the secret vault. The parchment-like paper rattled as he tugged it out.

He gave it a quick once-over to make sure it was a formula in Dr. Belorra's handwriting. He held back a whoop of pleasure.

His hand returned to the cubbyhole. His exploring fingers touched the black, gemlike pulsator that Cinnamon had planted. He stuffed pulsator, detector, and the Belorra formula into a pocket of his pantaloons.

From under his waistband, he yanked a folded paper that looked very much like the genuine formula. He dropped the phony into the vault with a little snap of his fingers. He couldn't help a quick grin. If the other side should ever follow the biochemical and mathematical puzzle on *that* piece of paper, they'd have to hold their noses to taste the mess!

Barney returned the bust to its place, and, with a quick glance at the guard, he hurried to the door. He opened it a crack. His luck was holding.

Then, when he stepped into the corridor, luck shattered into a million pieces. A guard rounded the ell and jerked to a stop at the sight of Barney.

"You, there! Where is Rabba? What are you doing in His Excellency's office?"

"I'm just on an errand." Barney laughed. "Rabba's in the office. Ask him yourself."

The guard hesitated. Barney kept cool and strode smoothly past.

"I'll do that," the guard decided with a dark frown.

As the guard opened the office door, Barney turned the ell and sprinted.

He broke outside just as he heard the guard's shouts in the building. Barney fought the tug of panic. It would take a minute or two, he reminded himself, for word to flash through the palace complex and for a search to be organized to hunt down an intruder.

He ran across an expanse of lawn and leaped a low hedge. Skirting the servants' quarters, he plunged past the rose arbor. Up in one of the minarets, a siren began to beep. The sound was much less frightful than the shouts and pounding footsteps of guards as they fanned across the grounds.

Barney ducked into the concealing shadows of the tropical garden. He dropped to his knees, his desperate hands searching the green sod for the trapdoor, which Willy would have carefully closed behind him and Dr. Belorra.

With a sinking sensation, Barney knew the seconds were too short. Far down the outer wall of the fortress, a searchlight winked on and began probing the darkly shadowed places about the grounds.

With a brief note of bitterness in his throat, Barney shut his thoughts from the hope of the secret passage under the wall. He couldn't risk having the finger of light nail him in the act of lifting the circle of sod and dropping from sight.

The light was swinging toward him. His eyes searched frantically. He jerked in a breath. A dozen yards away, a slender palm tree grew in a gentle curve close to the wall.

He ran to the tree, kicked off his sandals, clasped the trunk, and started climbing up. He poured strength into his straining muscles with the thought that he at least had one thing in his favor. The blazing light was seeking its prey behind a bush, cowering on the ground. If he could get above its level in time, he had a chance.

The grounds were quieter now, too quiet. The first moments of chaotic, shouted instructions were past. The searchers were covering the ground with cool efficiency.

The top of the wall swam in Barney's eye level. It looked as sharp as a knife—and inches too far away.

He blew a burning rivulet of sweat from the corner of his mouth and swung his weight against the top of the slender tree. It bowed a few feet away from the wall. When it swung back, Barney threw out his hands and shoved off with his feet.

He slammed against the top of the wall with an impact that jarred a sound of pain from him. He hung dizzily for a moment, his left elbow and right arm hooked over the rim. Clenching his teeth, he pulled himself up, rolled onto the top of the wall and lay flat, dragging deep, welcome breaths into his lungs.

He pressed down as the light searched the shadows directly below him.

When the light moved on, Barney inched himself over the outside of the wall. He hung by his finger-tips a moment before he pushed out with his feet and made the sickening drop.

11.   MAN IN
THE MIDDLE

CAPTAIN STEFAN ZOVOLOFF was beginning to show his steel. Knuckles on hips, arms akimbo, he towered over the desk in Aqaban's office.

Seated behind the desk, Aqaban continued his inner struggle at composure. For more than five minutes, he had suffered in silence while Zovoloff had come very close to calling him a double-dealing traitor.

"Wouldn't you say, Excellency"—Zovoloff's curling lips made a mockery of the title—"that some very strange things have been happening? First, the man —Phelps—shows up in the palace. Then Miriam Belorra appears. Next, while I'm present, Phelps barges into Miriam Belorra's room at the hotel like an old family friend. Finally, a prowler seemingly has the run of the palace itself. He comes and goes as if by magic. Perhaps," Zovoloff sneered, "he is from the fourth dimension and simply walks through the outer wall?"

Aqaban stared hard at the lapels of Zovoloff's suit to keep from meeting the foreign agent's eyes. He didn't want Zovoloff to see what might show in his own eyes if they locked stares.

Zovoloff paced back and forth. His movements made Aqaban think of a starving bear prowling after a winter's hibernation.

"Strangely enough," Zovoloff said, "the best your men can do is let this prowler get away clean and describe him only as a young Negro in Masacarian clothing."

The hint that the escape might have been arranged with collusion inside the palace was almost the final straw. Aqaban's neck swelled and pulsed with the effort to choke back his feelings. "I have men scouring the area. The search will continue until the young Negro is turned up. Before I'm through with him, he'll be only too glad to tell me how he got in the palace."

"I look forward to the interrogation," Zovoloff said. "Meanwhile, being occupied with the search, you will permit me to assist you in getting to the bottom of a few other things."

Aqaban shoved back his chair and stood up. An irate tremor shot through him. So the gloves were off, the sugar coating of diplomacy had dissolved. The dictator's mind nibbled at a suspicion. Had the palace prowler been a plant to give Zovoloff the excuse to put on the pressure?

"I would remind you," Aqaban said thickly, "that you are in Masacar."

"By your request." Zovoloff's voice was smooth. "You wanted a share of my country's power."

Aqaban stiffened. "I know your country could crush Masacar in a day. But you wouldn't dare. You couldn't risk the international reaction. I still rule here—and I don't like veiled threats."

"The threat isn't veiled, Excellency. I won't stand for both ends being played against the middle."

Aqaban's hawkish face burned red. He stabbed his thumb against his chest. "I'm not the one playing both ends. I'm the man being pushed into the middle!"

They looked at each other across the desk, tigerish but cautious.

"Then you will appreciate all the more not only my interest in your country's well-being, but in your personal welfare as well," Zovoloff said.

Aqaban stood with his hands clenching at his sides as Zovoloff moved to the corner of the desk and punched a button in the console.

"Yes, Excellency?" The response from the intercom was instant.

"This is Captain Stefan Zovoloff. His Excellency is ordering the arrest of Miriam Belorra. I'll personally take her in custody. Have a car ready to take me to the Hotel Ibn Lhaso."

The communicator hummed a short note of hesitancy. "As captain of the palace guard, I must have the arrest order from His Excellency."

Zovoloff raised from the bent position he had assumed to speak into the intercom. His eyes drilled into Aqaban's.

Inwardly the dictator seethed in a welter of emotion, outrage, frustration, and a sudden burst of dark fear. He felt suddenly like an exhausted swimmer who could not find a solid bottom under his toes.

"Well, Excellency?" Zovoloff's voice was icy.

"Of course I had thought of talking to the girl myself, but I was delayed when you barged in," Aqaban bit out the lamely face-saving words. He leaned toward the communicator. "You have my permission to accept Captain Zovoloff's orders temporarily."

"Acknowledged, Excellency," the voice intoned from the intercom. "The car will be ready."

When Aqaban raised up, Zovoloff was smiling. His eyes glinted with their usual reserved coolness, but the ice had melted. "There, my friend, you see how easy it is to unravel a misunderstanding. We simply have to know where we stand, don't we?"

Aqaban didn't trust himself to speak. Zovoloff saw this. He sensed Aqaban's feelings, now that the upstart found himself standing in the shadow of a smarter and more powerful man.

Zovoloff was immune to sympathy or pity. Let Aqaban stew. He had missed his chance to keep the driver's seat a moment ago when he had hissed an assent into the communicator.

He rendered Aqaban a short mock bow. "I'll rejoin

you soon, Excellency," he said as he strode out.

A big black sedan was waiting outside with a chauffeur snapping to attention and opening the door for Zovoloff.

The driver slid behind the steering wheel and put the car in purring movement around the front courtyard.

"The hotel, Captain?"

Zovoloff glanced at the back of the driver's shoulders and head. "Yes—but first the airport. I want to make sure my pilot isn't sneaking into the city to see the sights."

He knew the driver would report the detour to Aqaban. The explanation wouldn't satisfy the upstart, but it would give him something to accept.

The car stopped for clearance at the front gate. Then it was outside, jouncing along the rutted road that skirted the archaeological diggings.

Zovoloff idly noted two shadowy figures plodding along in the night far across the diggings. For a brief moment they were objects of his curiosity and speculation. Then he shrugged. They were doubtless a pair of half-starved peasants reworking the sifted dirt at the edge of the diggings in hopes of finding a bit of bric-a-brac worth a few coppers.

Other things quickly erased the distant figures from his mind. Not once did it occur to him that one of the figures was Dr. Hasman Belorra.

He clicked on the dome light, drew a notebook and pencil from the inner pocket of his suit jacket, and spent the rest of the trip to the airport coding a message. It advised his superiors that Aqaban was acting in questionable faith.

The limousine made a final turn. The headlights flared across the dark administration building and touched the tarmac beyond, where Zovoloff's jet crouched like a silver bullet with stubby wings. Noting the disuse of the building, the little fantails of sand stirred by the lonely breeze, the weeds growing along the runways, Zovoloff's lips curled in disdain. The airport predicted the fate of Aqaban. In due time, the man would go. The airport would live again, to the sound of military jets and workers ringing the area with missile sites.

The car braked in the shadow of the jet's fuselage. Zovoloff got out and looked up into the menace of a submachine gun snouting from a cabin window.

"It's your captain," Zovoloff said.

The weapon was withdrawn. Zovoloff walked to the cabin door. As it opened, he handed up the message he had coded. The pilot reached down to take it. He understood that Zovoloff wasn't alone. He didn't need spoken instructions to radio the message right away.

"How is it going?" Zovoloff remarked.

"Very quiet, sir. The galley is well provisioned, the aircraft comfortable quarters."

"Good. Stand by on red-alert status."

"I understand, sir."

The cabin door closed while Zovoloff was taking the few steps back to the car.

Zovoloff settled in the rear seat and relaxed during

the ride into the heart of the city.

He was speculating about the various futures that could be arranged for Aqaban when the driver announced arrival at the Ibn Lhaso.

Zovoloff stepped out on the sidewalk, the driver holding the car door open. Traffic was a mere trickle on the wide street. A few people straggled along the sidewalks. The air of decay and desertion, of hopeless despair, seemed to be creeping throughout Masacar under Aqaban's tyranny.

A dirty beggar in rags scurried out of Zovoloff's way as the captain moved from the official-looking car to the hotel entry.

Ignoring the desk clerk and idle bell captain, Zovoloff strode to the elevator. He rode up and walked directly to the door of the Miriam Belorra suite.

He listened, ear against the door. He heard her movements inside. His knuckles beat a peremptory summons.

The door was opened by the dark-skinned, black-haired personal maid. She seemed startled by Zovoloff's appearance.

"Is Miss Belorra in?" Zovoloff's inquiry was courteous.

"Who is it, Lara?" a young woman's voice called from one of the bedrooms.

"Captain Stefan Zovoloff, Miss Belorra." He raised the level of his voice.

Cinnamon Carter came into the sitting room. She was wearing a simple, attractive print dress. "I was just changing to go out to dinner. But do come in."

Zovoloff stepped past the maid, and Cinnamon came forward, a nag of worry in her eyes. "Captain, is it about my father? Is he all right?"

"Nothing has happened to your father, Miss Belorra."

The tightness flew from Cinnamon's shoulders with an expelled breath. She managed a smile and offered her hand. "Then your visit isn't unwelcome, Captain." She glanced past Zovoloff. "Lara, you may be excused. Have a pleasant evening—but do be careful."

"Yes, Miss Belorra." Miriam, in the guise of Lara, curtsied and walked out quietly, closing the door gently.

Zovoloff had no interest in a personal maid. One in her circumstance didn't rate a second glance.

Cinnamon idled across the room, looked at herself in a wall mirror, and touched the lipstick at the corner of her mouth with the tip of her little finger.

"What brings you here, Captain?" Her eyes caught his in the mirror. "Has Mr. Aqaban decided to release my father?"

"Is that what you talked about?"

Cinnamon's brows lifted. "He didn't tell you?" A faint smile caught her lips. "Perhaps you should ask him what we talked about."

"I intend to ask you both," Zovoloff said, "at the palace."

She froze for a second, then turned slowly to face him. "Am I being arrested, Captain?"

"Why use the word? Just say that I'm inviting you to the palace."

Her eyes held on his face. She seemed to be study-ing him. Actually, she was wondering if she should try stalling so that Miriam Belorra would have enough time to get clear of the hotel.

"For dinner, Captain?" Cinnamon smiled.

"If you like." A stiffness was slipping into his voice. He was impatient. She had no choice about going to the palace, and he was about ready to point out the fact.

"I'd intended to sample local food in a nearby café." She glanced down at herself. "I'm not exactly dressed for a meal at the palace."

"We're not going to a formal banquet, Miss Belorra. Your outfit will do."

"Very well." Her eyes grew moody. A shiver touched her shoulders. "I might as well face up to the established fact of arrest, hadn't I? I really don't de-serve it, though. All I've done is come back to my homeland."

"The experience need not be unpleasant, Miss Be-lorra." Zovoloff could afford the courtesy of holding the door for her, now that he was experiencing so little difficulty. "No one wants to make it that way. It depends on you."

Zovoloff maintained a thoughtful silence during the ride back to the palace and the walk into Aqaban's office.

Aqaban's eyes shot a fierce warning for Cinnamon not to reveal that he had toyed with the idea of a double cross during her previous visit.

The dictator had the look of a rat trapped in a maze

of its own making. But he managed a cock-of-the-walk stance behind his desk.

Zovoloff strode to Aqaban's side. Instead of speaking to Aqaban, however, he punched a button on the desk console.

"Yes, Excellency?" the robot-like voice responded.

"Bring Dr. Belorra here—at once!"

Zovoloff straightened and nodded Cinnamon to a chair. He watched her sink slowly. "I think we'll fill in a few gaps shortly," he said.

"I think we're wasting time." Aqaban's voice was sullen. "Miss Belorra's motives are easily understood. She's a young girl who became heartsick for her father. Knowing he was imprisoned, her own freedom was a torment. The father-daughter attachment drove her back. She simply had to try to do something for him."

"She wouldn't have been much of a daughter if she hadn't wanted to help her father," Zovoloff agreed.

"Naturally," Aqaban said.

"And naturally you've overlooked one point—or you're keeping quiet about it." Zovoloff's sharp gaze picked at the tight and slightly damp details of Aqaban's face. "She would plan and make preparations before she returned."

Aqaban's lips parted on a short, empty laugh. "You're jumping at shadows."

"We'll see."

Zovoloff seated himself on the edge of the desk, watching the door for the appearance of the prisoner. His cool silence gnawed at Aqaban. The dictator remained standing, his hands toying restlessly with objects on the desk—the letter opener, a gold-cased pen.

Cinnamon jumped from the chair when the office door opened. Rollin was framed there. He stumbled slightly as the guard who had brought him up gave him a shove from behind.

Cinnamon ran to Rollin and threw her arms about him. She drew back and held him at arm's length. "Are you all right, Papa?"

"Yes, yes." He glared at Aqaban and Zovoloff. Zovoloff's penetrating eyes watched the meeting closely.

Rollin slipped the protection of his arm about Cinnamon's shoulders. He had certainly worked his unbelievable wizardry in his appearance. He looked and sounded so much like Dr. Belorra that possibly even the real Miriam wouldn't have quickly detected the difference.

"I won't stand for any threats directed at my daughter!" he warned.

Zovoloff motioned for the guard to step back to the door.

"Relax, Doctor." Zovoloff pulled away from the desk. His stern Nordic face permitted a smile. His conservative suit, white shirt, and neatly knotted necktie suggested an executive calling a board meeting to order. "All I want at the moment is a few answers."

"I'm not sure I have them," Rollin said.

Zovoloff clasped his hands quietly behind his back. "Well, let's try them and see. We'll begin with a man named Phelps. He's registered at the Ibn Lhaso. Miss

Belorra seems to know him."

"Our paths happened to cross as we were both entering the dining room," Cinnamon said. "We spoke and. . . ."

"I'm not asking you, Miss Belorra. I want to know if your father also knows him." Zovoloff didn't miss Rollin's slight hesitation. "I think the question could be more properly put, Doctor. How long have you known Phelps?"

"I have heard of the man," Rollin admitted.

"During one of your visits to Rome?"

"Well . . . yes." Rollin nodded. "I believe his name was spoken there."

"Who is he, Doctor? What does he do?"

"I understand his activities are varied," Rollin said. "I've heard that he represents some kind of international organization."

Behind the desk, Aqaban eased into his chair with twitching muscles. His eyes blazed an order for Rollin to shut up. But Rollin's attention was all on the man standing just in front of the corner of the desk.

"Does Phelps know anything about your work?" Zovoloff asked.

Rollin shrugged. "Several people in Italy, in academic and scientific circles, knew that the protein research was making its difficult and tedious way."

"If Phelps's international organization was on the lookout for new industrial patents, scientific breakthroughs, mineral and oil discoveries . . . in short, if Phelps represents a capitalistic cartel, could he have learned about your research?"

"It's possible."

"Isn't it also possible," Zovoloff insisted, "that Phelps might have deduced, from your forcible detention in Masacar, that you had achieved a breakthrough?"

"If Phelps was interested," Rollin said, "it must have been clear to him that His Excellency wouldn't go to the trouble of holding me for nothing."

Aqaban sat stiffly on the edge of his desk chair. His eyes daggered Zovoloff's broad back.

Zovoloff took a step from the desk. His cool executive look underwent a subtle change. His shoulders assumed a menacing thrust.

Looking into Zovoloff's face, Rollin edged Cinnamon slightly behind him with the pressure of his hand.

"I want a careful answer to my next question, Doctor," Zovoloff cautioned. "Have you talked with Phelps recently?"

"Yes, I have."

"Where?"

"In the cell downstairs. His Excellency"—Rollin's eyes were bitter—"needed to show proof that he really had me. I was the prize animal in the cage."

Zovoloff, looking deep into Rollin's eyes, exhaled a long breath. "Thank you, Doctor." He glanced at the guard and snapped a motion with his hand. "Return Dr. Belorra to his cell."

The guard marched to Rollin's side and took hold of Rollin's arm.

"By the way," Zovoloff added, as if on afterthought, "Miss Belorra will visit her father for a while."

Rollin jerked about, almost breaking the guard's

grip. "You can't throw her into that rotten hole!"

With a quick look at Zovoloff, Cinnamon ran to Rollin.

"No, Father. Don't irritate the man right now. He isn't in the mood for it. You'll make things worse."

Her voice had a calming effect on Rollin. She looked back at Zovoloff. "He's a valuable man. Remember that!"

"Quite, Miss Belorra." Zovoloff made an insulting bow as the guard herded them out.

Zovoloff turned slowly to Aqaban. The dictator's skittish gaze avoided Zovoloff's eyes. His face was perplexed. In a man of Aqaban's disposition, Zovoloff knew, uncertainties were as dangerous as sparking dynamite fuses.

Zovoloff studied the man behind the desk for a long moment. Aqaban broke the silence with a clearing of his throat, but he didn't speak. He was playing it with the cunning of a fox seeing the shadow of a hound over its hole. He was offering no explanations to give Zovoloff an entering wedge.

"A column of figures can add up to only one answer," Zovoloff said finally.

"Unless the bookkeeper makes an error."

"The true answer is nevertheless the same—once the error is discovered."

"I wasn't referring to myself." Aqaban squirmed slightly in his chair.

"So I have made an error?" Zovoloff coaxed icily.

"How can I know, until you've told me your answer?"

"The facts speak for themselves." Zovoloff paced back and forth in front of the desk. "Phelps appears in Masacar as if he had popped from the sands. The girl returns. They know each other too well to have just met in the hotel. Both are interested in the same man, Dr. Hasman Belorra. Nobody but a fool would believe it all to be accidental. It dovetails too well to be anything but a prearranged plan."

The lids hooding Aqaban's eyes looked as if they had been oiled. He started to say something, then changed his mind. He watched his fingertip trace the sharp edge of the letter opener as he waited.

"It's all perfectly clear," Zovoloff went on. "It could have happened in only one way. The cartel represented by Phelps wants to get its hands on the Belorra formula. Phelps contacted Miriam Belorra in Rome and outlined his deal. He slipped her out—a jump ahead of my agents. He wanted her help in selling you on the deal. She went along because it offered hope for her father."

"Deal?" Aqaban muttered.

"A very enticing deal, I would imagine." Zovoloff paused to give emphasis to his words. "With its limitless millions in finance capital, a cartel could develop the Belorra process right here in Masacar."

A dryness burned through Aqaban's throat. The shadow of the pacing man swept across the desk. Aqaban was awed by Zovoloff's deductive and reasoning powers.

Then Aqaban braced himself. Zovoloff was flesh and blood, he reminded himself. Anyone in possession of the basic facts couldn't have reasoned to any other conclusion. Zovoloff wasn't such a genius, just lucky enough to have the important pieces fall in his lap.

Aqaban knew that Zovoloff was waiting for him to speak. He deliberately let several seconds pass. This was still Masacar, and he was Janar Aqaban, the man in control.

At last he raised his eyes to Zovoloff's. "You're convinced now that I have what I said I had? The man in the cell is really Dr. Belorra? I do have the formula?"

Zovoloff pressed the heels of his palms on the desk and leaned forward. "I'm convinced it's time I had a look at the formula. Otherwise, I might think you were considering a deal with the cartel."

Reluctantly, Aqaban forced himself out of the chair. He could think of no reasonable excuse for further delay while his unwilling feet carried him to the wall niche.

He grasped the statue, wriggled it loose on its beveled base, and lifted it out. His other hand dipped into the compartment beneath. He lifted out the folded paper, and Zovoloff snatched it from his hand.

Zovoloff quickly uncreased the paper. He began studying the long and involved series of figures and symbols.

Aqaban watched the movement of Zovoloff's eyes. Then, as his gaze strayed to the blank backside of the paper, Aqaban stopped breathing. For a second he was dizzy, faint. Nothing was real except the texture and quality of the paper, so unlike the vellum on which a genius, under truth drugs, had surrendered his discovery.

Zovoloff's face swam back into focus. He refolded the paper and stood tapping it against his thumbnail. "The paper sets forth a rather bizarre manipulation of the heavy nitrogenous molecule," he admitted. "The latter results are not clear. The math and biochemical levels become specialized. But we'll see what cooks up—in a laboratory."

Aqaban reached for the formula, but Zovoloff slipped it smoothly aside.

"I think, Comrade," Zovoloff said, "that the formula is a fake. If so, you had better remember where you have the genuine one hidden!"

Dazed, Aqaban watched Zovoloff stride from the office, the formula disappearing into the pocket of his jacket.

Aqaban looked at the small marble bust he was still holding. He threw it hard against the carpet and stumbled toward the desk.

The prowler who had been in the palace took on a deeper and more frightening dimension. Zovoloff's man? A cog in a scheme to steal the real formula and then have the excuse to abandon the leader of a nation too poor to be anything but a liability?

An agent paid by Phelps?

Someone recruited by Miriam Belorra in Rome?

Whoever the young Negro was, how had he known where to look for the formula?

The wild questions cascaded through Aqaban's mind with an acid bite. He sleeved sweat from his eyes, staining the pure white of his uniform. With a trembling hand, he stabbed a console button.

"Yes, Excellency?"

"Redouble efforts to catch the young Negro who was seen in the palace," he snarled. "Make it clear to your men that I'll fill the shackles and cells in the dungeon if they let him get away!"

"Right away, Your Excellency!"

Aqaban flopped into his chair. He hooked his finger under his collar and tugged it loose. But he still felt as if he were choking.

12.   REUNION

FOR HIS LOOKOUT POST, Jim Phelps had chosen the rubble of a ruined rock garden several yards from the Belorra house. A friendly eucalyptus tree threw shadows that swallowed him. From it, if necessity arose, he could move in almost any direction across the estate. Yet the tree didn't obstruct his view of that lonely and forlorn house and its approaches.

He had skipped dinner, and that didn't particularly bother him. The continual silence did.

Then the cracking of a twig burst through his nerves. His gaze swept the moon-bathed field east of the battered house. He saw the dark silhouette of a human figure disappear briefly in the shadows of a pepper tree. As moonlight glistened on the black hair and dark-dyed facial features, Phelps hurried to meet Miriam Belorra. The rustle of tough weeds mingled with the girl's exhausted breathing.

"Jim," she gasped. Her running feet faltered. Strength had drained from her knees and she stumbled. Phelps leaped forward to catch her.

His grip on her elbow steadied her. She could do nothing more for a moment than stand there and let her burning lungs fight for breath.

"Ran so hard . . . to tell you. . ." she gasped. "Cinnamon . . . she's in trouble."

"Easy," Jim said. He helped Miriam to a low, vine-grown stone wall near the eucalyptus tree and eased her to a sitting position.

"First thing, get your breath back so you can tell me," he said.

Even as she nodded, her breath returned. "That man . . . not Aqaban . . . the other one. . . ."

"Zovoloff."

"Yes, he came to the hotel. To our rooms without warning. He placed Cinnamon under arrest, of course thinking she was me." Miriam's face worked. Her fingers gripped his forearm. "Jim, he has taken her to the palace, and if anything happens to her because she is wearing my face . . . well, I'd never forgive myself."

He took her hand in both of his. "You've been through a long stretch of trouble, Miriam. But hang on a while longer. Don't let it break your nerve. Danger is part of the game. Cinnamon knows that as well as any of us. We went into this thing with our eyes wide open. You're not to blame, whatever happens."

"You talk sense," she admitted. She raised her fingertips to her heart. "But this is where I feel—and sense talk doesn't always change it."

"You're exhausted," Jim said. "Come on into the house. I've a jug of fresh water that should help."

She got up, steadily enough, and preceded Jim across the garden and along the dark portico where the masonry was chipped and weeds were ferreting out cracks up through the tile.

They turned into the small back room, and when he had closed the door Jim crossed to the heavy, hanging blanket and double-checked the makeshift blackout curtain. Then he turned on a small electric torch, picked up a moisture-beaded canteen, and handed it to Miriam.

Between thirsty gulps, she detailed Zovoloff's arrival and Cinnamon's arrest.

"You have any trouble getting away?" Jim asked.

"No, Cinnamon was very clever with that. She simply excused me. She was so natural, so normal. She did it in such a way that Zovoloff didn't give a second look at a commonplace maid." Her lips quivered. Looking at Jim, her eyes suddenly swam with tears. "It was so easy for me, Jim. But on the way here my thoughts became clearer. Shouldn't I have stayed? Gone with her? Be there if it's necessary to prove to them that she really isn't Miriam Belorra?"

Jim circled her shoulders with his arm. "On the way here," he corrected, "your thoughts became confused.

If you were there and proved to them that you were Miriam Belorra, would it really help Cinnamon? Rather, wouldn't it just throw all the fat in the fire?"

She studied his face for a moment. "I'm afraid I'm out of my depth, Jim. In water where I've never learned the right swimming stroke. But I'll follow orders. I won't do anything foolish."

"I know that," Jim said. "You've proven it already. Zovoloff is putting on the squeeze, but he may end up finding it on himself. We're not through with him and Mr. Aqaban just yet."

Jim broke off as a rapping on the door resounded softly through the room. The knuckle of a bent finger beat a dot-dot-dash-dot-dot code.

Jim spun away from Miriam and picked up the torch. The glow caught his quick smile in the instant before he plunged the room into darkness. "May be a little out of season," he said, "but get set for the best Christmas present of your life."

He was a rustle of sound as he crossed the room and opened the door. Two shadowy figures slipped inside. Jim closed the door, the latch snicking. Then, with a burst of anticipation, he clicked the button of the electric lantern.

The light showered Dr. Belorra and Willy. Jim looked at Miriam's face. For a moment she couldn't speak or move. Neither could Dr. Belorra trust his own voice. Miriam took a first halting step as he held out his arms. "Father?" The word was a choked sob of joy. Then her clutching arms were about him, and Dr. Belorra enveloped her.

She buried her face against his shoulder, emotion storming through her. Dr. Belorra's eyes were wet with tears. He stroked her hair, content just to hold her, the strong young woman who was nevertheless still his little girl.

Miriam lifted her tear-streaked face. She freed a hand to touch his cheek. To her, his prison pallor was vivid. "Father, have they hurt you so. . . ."

He smothered her words with a booming laugh. "I'm fine, girl, just fine! You didn't really think they could clip the mane of this old lion, did you?"

He held her at arm's length, his face glowing. "What is this? The skin color? The hair? The changes? I'd hardly know you if I passed you on the street. But of course Mr. Armitage told me what to expect as we made our way here."

"Let's hope the disguise can be shucked soon," Willy said, "in a friendlier climate."

Dr. Belorra nodded. Willy's words posed the really big question in Dr. Belorra's mind. The final hurdle seemed to him the highest, the most impossible. Successes achieved inside Masacar were meaningless without the ultimate success—escape. Marooned in Masacar . . . the alliterative phrase burned through Dr. Belorra's mind. Just how did Phelps propose to get all of these people out of a land locked tight by a dictator?

The question was on the tip of Dr. Belorra's tongue, but Miriam's slender presence held it back. Right now the girl could think only of one thing. Her father was here, real and solid before her eyes, warm and substantial to the arm she slipped about him. *Give her this moment,* Dr. Belorra thought, *this one moment of sheer happiness, however blind. She'll think of the big question herself, quickly enough. Don't remind her now that this may be the only such moment she has.*

Willy cleared his throat. "I know you and Miriam would like to have some time for a long talk, Doctor. But this is just a way stop. We'd better be on our way."

"We're ready," Dr. Belorra said.

Miriam held out her hand to Jim. "Are you coming with us?"

"I'll join you later." Jim's fingers met her firm clasp.

Her eyes filled with expression. "Jim, they haven't yet invented the words I need to thank you. Even if we should fail to get out, this has been the best moment of my life."

"I've rather enjoyed being part of it myself." Jim smiled. "Now off with you. Willy will have you safely dug in by the time Dr. Belorra's absence is discovered."

Jim extinguished the torch. Willy opened the door, framing a patch of night glow. The shadows of Dr. Belorra, Miriam, and Willy flowed outside. Jim stood in the doorway, watching their vague movement along the portico, listening to the soft sounds of their flight. Silence crept in. They melted into the darkness.

Phelps closed the door and moved into the portico shadows. He padded through the darkness and returned to his lookout post. He stood beside the low stone wall, his eyes searching hard in all directions.

His forehead surrendered to a heavy frown. He drew in a tight breath. He couldn't any longer duck the fact that Barney Collier was late. Barney was off schedule. Barney had run into trouble.

Then Jim gave a long sigh of relief as he saw the figure of a man in baggy pantaloons limned in the moonlit inner courtyard. He was a flickering mirage, quickly gone. Barney Collier was very good at moving without being seen.

Jim returned to the portico and slipped to the doorway of the room they had chosen as the homing point, the temporary headquarters.

He lifted his hand and rapped out the code on the wooden panel. The door eased a crack, then swung wide. Jim stepped inside, and Barney closed the door.

The torch flared in Barney's hand. In its subdued glow, his black face was sweaty, dusty, stamped with tiredness. He limped slightly as he moved across the room. He plopped awkwardly on a broken chair and stretched out his left leg. Bending forward, he massaged his calf.

With a movement of quick concern, Jim dropped to one knee beside him.

Barney turned his head slightly to flash a grin. "Pulled muscle," he explained. "But nothing broken. I had to shinny a tree and drop from the top of the palace wall."

The concern eased in Jim's eyes.

"I had the tough luck to run into a guard on my way out of Aqaban's office," Barney explained. "Couldn't use the aqueduct without the risk of tipping off Aqaban. Thank goodness for that tree!"

He stood up, stamping his foot, working his leg up and down. "They're really beating the bushes for me, Jim. One of them almost stepped on me as he and a couple of pals searched an alley not far from the palace. It complicates things. But—" His smile gleamed wolfishly. He slid a crackling piece of paper from the concealment of his pantaloons and dangled it before Jim's eyes. "How do you like them apples?"

Jim took the parchment-like oblong and unfolded it. His eyes seemed to gather the torch's light as he scanned the Belorra formula. He glanced at Barney, grinning.

"I'd say them apples are choice, Barney!"

Barney settled on the chair and resumed the leg massage while he watched Jim.

Phelps spread the formula on the floor, reached for the electric lantern, and spread its full glow across the vellum.

His hand dipped into his trousers pocket and came out holding a small alligator key case. He pulled the zipper, clipped open the case, and a mini-camera fell into his other hand.

With the camera at his right eye, he focused and microfilmed the formula. He reset the camera and repeated the action.

Without speaking, he snapped open the camera and handed the tiny roll to Barney. Then Jim picked a second tiny cartridge from the key case between the tips of his thumb and middle finger. He reloaded the camera, bent toward the formula, and recorded it on two more frames. He raised and replaced the camera in its bogus case.

He and Barney looked at each other. Both shared the thought. If either got out, so would a microfilm.

"We'll get out, together," Barney said quietly.

Jim nodded. "But if not, we've got insurance now. If either of us gets out, the free world will have a look at Dr. Belorra's sweet apples."

Jim again crouched. He stretched out his hand and curled a corner of the vellum up away from the floor. He fished a book of paper matches from his suit coat pocket, struck one, and touched the tiny flame to the formula.

In silence, he and Barney watched it burn. When it was a brittle, blackened ash, Jim stood up and scattered the charcoal dust with his foot.

Barney clambered up from the chair with a very slight wince.

"Sure the leg's okay?" Jim asked.

"Old Charley's horse has about quit bucking."

"We could make a small change of plan if you. . . ."

"Daddy-O!" Barney's lifted hand was a request for silence. "You think the show is going on with Mrs. Collier's little boy tucked in offstage?"

Jim's playful jab thumped against Barney's shoulder.

"I'm glad you didn't break it. I'd probably have to tote you in piggyback."

"Just to where the action is," Barney said. "Man, let's get moving. We going to stick around here until we get old? That's not for me."

The touchy trip through the dark back streets of Masarium was stop and go, crouch, duck, and hide. The search for Barney had spread over the city. Jeep-like vehicles cruised with probing spotlights. Gray army trucks spilled teams of strong-arm searchers.

Block by block, Jim and Barney worked their way toward the palace minarets, beacons bathed in golden light against the night sky.

A crackle of distant, angry shouts drifted to Barney and Jim.

"Wow!" Barney breathed. "Sounds like some citizens are grabbing the chance to show how sick and tired they are of Aqaban."

Underscoring his words, a rifle cracked somewhere across the city.

"Aqaban's overdue for an eye-opener," Jim said.

He flopped with Barney behind a garbage can as a finger of light stabbed through the alley. The light washed over the walls of mud-brick buildings, testing the innocent silence of the alley. The glow faded as a slowly moving truck trundled onward.

Jim and Barney raised up slowly.

"Close," Barney whispered.

"We're less than half a mile from the palace," Jim mused.

"Think it's time we made our move?"

"I think," Jim said.

"Then what are we waiting for?"

They worked their way along the wall to a point a few feet from the street.

"Okay," Jim whispered, "we're in business."

Barney seemed to stretch into invisibility at the base of the wall.

Jim stepped out to the edge of the dusty street. He surveyed the block quickly. He guessed that normally the bedraggled artisan's stalls and food shops stayed open as long as hope for another customer remained. Tonight, with Aqaban's guards roaming, most of the places had already closed. Here and there a light showed in the stall of a weaver, potter, or leather worker who lived with his family in a space to the rear.

Jim dawdled to a narrow store where a dusty window displayed straw sandals and hats, unglazed water jugs, small prayer rugs.

He idled, killing several impatient minutes.

A flare of light at the intersection caught his quick attention. One of the jeep-type cars slowed at the corner and turned.

Jim's muscles tightened. He stepped into the headlight glare and lifted his hand.

In obedience to his signal, the jeep bucked to a stop, its wheels puffing clouds of dust. Jim's white skin wasn't suspicious. His custom-cut business suit was out of place, but his demeanor was convincingly innocent.

The jeep held two men. The guardsman beside the driver stood up. He was middle-aged, burly, with a huge black moustache. The jeep creaked under the shifting of his weight. "What's the trouble? Lost?"

"Hardly," Jim said. With quiet, easy motion he dissolved the short distance between himself and the driver's side. "My name is Phelps. Member of a business mission. I'm registered at the Ibn Lhaso."

"What are you doing over here in this section?" the burly man asked.

Jim's brows flipped up, as if the question didn't entirely make sense. "Why, I'm not exactly a stranger. I'm a friend of your country and like to learn about it. And"—the hint of greed in his smile was something the guards could understand—"I'm always on the lookout for sidelines I can turn into a personal profit." He hooked a thumb over his shoulder. "Such as the handtooled leather work in the shops over there. Unfortunately, they have closed for the night."

"Good reason. There's been some trouble."

"Yes," Jim nodded. "I've heard. You're looking for a young Negro who escaped the palace."

"And we're running into more than just that," the burly man glowered. "You should be off the streets. The hotel is the best place for foreign visitors right now."

"I'm anxious to get there," Jim said, "but first I felt I should tell someone in authority. I noticed a man drag himself into the alley. Is the Negro hurt?"

"Perhaps." The burly man's voice tightened. "The fool dropped from the palace wall."

"Then it wouldn't surprise me one bit," Jim said, "if you find your culprit nursing his sprains in the alley. He hasn't had time to get away."

The driver eased the jeep in gear. He was slow to let out the clutch.

"This should be quite a feather in your caps," Jim prodded. "I've an upcoming appointment with His Excellency as a member of my trade mission. Perhaps I could mention your names?"

"Dabuul and Nasivar," the driver said, taking the pressure of his foot from the clutch.

Jim stayed beside the vehicle as it inched forward and nosed into the alley. The headlights swept the narrow canyon to its dead end against the back of a building facing the next block.

"You must have been mistaken," the driver said. "I see nothing."

"How about that garbage can?" Jim suggested. "Maybe he's hiding behind it."

Both guards looked at the battered container halfway down the alley. Jim glimpsed Barney rising from prone invisibility at the corner of the building. Both guards sensed movement in almost the same instant. They turned, caught a fleeting look at the materializing black shadow, and grabbed at the pistols holstered at their sides.

Jim ducked, holding his breath. He heard the sharp hiss as Barney pointed a small vial of nerve gas and let the guards have it full in their faces.

The guards slumped, bumping together in an unconscious sprawl. Still holding his breath, Jim reached to the instrument panel and switched off the headlights. He flipped open the door, grabbed the driver by the shoulders, and dragged him out. Barney was doing the same with the other guard.

With a soft grunt or two, Jim and Barney shoul-

dered the men, fireman fashion, and carried them
along the alley. They stretched out the two guards
behind the garbage can.

Straightening up, Barney said, "Have a good nap,
fellows. You'll wake up none the worse for wear."

Jim remained bent over the driver a moment longer,
stripping off the limp man's tunic. As he trotted back
to the jeep Jim yanked the tunic on over his suit
jacket. The fit was terrible, and he would swelter in
so much clothing. But the cut was right, the color
proper, the buttons brass, if he had to raise his hand
in passing greeting.

The guard's peaked cap had fallen beside the jeep.
Jim brushed it off and slipped it on.

Barney clambered over the seats and curled out of
sight in space behind. Jim wriggled under the steering wheel, started the jeep, and turned on the lights.

The tires squealed as Phelps cut the wheel and
swung the jeep around in the middle of the street.
Then, like a frisky colt, the jeep raced off in the direction of the palace.

CONFIDENTIAL
13. CONVERSATION

PHELPS BRAKED the jeep beneath the straggly palm tree which, by day, afforded shade to the bulky overseer of the diggers at the archaeological site.

"Come on out and stretch a muscle," Jim said.

Barney raised up in back, threw a leg over, and slid into the seat beside Jim.

Phelps looked at the shadowed acres of disrupted earth, the black bands that marked trenches, the darkness like black rivers along the base of terraces.

"Hang on," Jim said, his eyes picking out a spot ahead.

He ran the jeep in low to the edge of a shallow trench and eased the nose over. The rear end slipped for a precarious moment when the jeep tilted steeply down. Jim inched the steering wheel to the left. The jeep straightened and began crawling with its four-wheel drive down the shallow slope like a caterpillar, its headlights off.

The jeep settled level, and Jim turned off the ignition.

"If that overseer does his nocturnal prowling tonight," Barney said, leaping out over the side, "he might get ideas about offering a jeep as a black-market item."

"He'd have to stand right there on the edge of the slope to see it," Jim said. "Even then he'd almost have to be looking for it, dark as it is in the cut. He probably will stay close to home tonight, with so many guards nosing through the byways. Anyway, we'll have to play the odds that the jeep won't be discovered."

He followed Barney to the top of the short slope, where Barney paused to reconnoiter the diggings with a slow, careful gaze.

"All clear," Barney said. "Nothing on deck tonight but us ground squirrels."

Jim peeled off the guard tunic and took off the peaked cap. He rolled the cap in the tunic and tossed the bundle down beside the jeep.

"Our subway turnstile is right over here," Barney said.

He set off across the mounds and ridges of loose earth at a trot, Jim hard on his heels.

Barney's pace slackened. "Watch your step."

As if to add emphasis to his words, Barney slid out of sight. Jim picked his way down the angled side of the trench, throwing out his hand to steady himself as his feet slipped and spilled a small avalanche into the dark depths.

Jim rocked to a halt in the bottom of the trench. A few feet away, Barney was a dark form dropping to his knees. His quick hands brushed away loose dirt and small stones that covered the thin stone slab.

"Upsy-daisy, Jim."

Jim dug his fingers under the side of the slab. He and Barney lifted the stone between them a few inches, then pushed it to one side. Exposed was the dark rupture in the old Roman aqueduct.

Barney raised up. From a pocket in his baggy pantaloons, he fished a small package, a little thicker than a man's wallet.

The item was fold after fold of tissue-thin plastic. Its rustling was a soft whisper as Jim shook it out. Extended to its full length and width, it resembled the protective covering in which a dry cleaner returns a topcoat.

"No cracks about my Mother Hubbard coveralls," Jim warned, his fingers separating the clinging layers at the bottom, the armholes, and the neck opening.

"I should disparage a guy who wants to keep his suit natty so's he can stroll through the palace without looking like he's been dragged out of the cellar?" Barney grinned. He reached to assist Jim as he pulled the garment over his head. Together they wriggled the clinging film down the length of Jim's body. It covered him from neck to calves. He crackled softly with each movement.

"You'll crawl hot in that thing," Barney said, "but it's the mod style this year for dust-free crawling through two-thousand-year-old Roman aqueducts."

"Spare me the corn," Jim groaned, "and dive in."

Lowering himself into the tunnel, Barney said, "I'll give us a light when we're far enough inside."

Barney ducked out of sight. Jim gave him time to get half a dozen feet ahead, then sat on the edge of the hole, hands braced on the sides.

Easing himself down, Jim heard Barney's slithering movements in a darkness so dense it rendered human eyes totally blind.

Jim crouched, feeling the pitted stone under his palms and tasting the increasing staleness of the air. It brought an unpleasant memory of the time several years before when, for a hairy hour, he'd thought he was lost in the maze of an Egyptian pyramid.

The going was easier when Barney snapped on a pen light, creating a faint, rosy haze ahead.

Barney stopped at last and turned in a crouch as Jim closed the gap.

Barney flicked the light beam in the hole over his head.

"Our exit," he said. "A nice little manhole covered with green sod. Keep your fingers crossed that a guard's big feet aren't planted on it."

"My fingers have been crossed," Jim whispered back. "Let's hope a big part of the palace guard has been drawn off to help in the citywide search for that mysterious young Negro roaming the area."

Barney clicked off the light. Jim heard him stir. Several seconds passed while Barney stretched and cautiously lifted the sod trapdoor. A faint fog of light seeped down from the palace grounds.

Jim inched forward and looked up. He saw the round, moonlike opening. Uncoiling, he brushed bits of dirt from the sides of the hole. He hooked his hands over the edge, dug in with his toes, and hauled himself up. As his shoulders appeared, he was given a boost by Barney's hands.

Standing in the shadows beside Barney, Jim took hold of the plastic film at the neck opening. He ripped it away. It had served its purpose. He wadded it and dropped it in the manhole while he studied what he could see of the palace through rifts in the tropical greenery.

Barney had dropped to his knee to ease the sod trapdoor tenderly in place. He raised and touched Jim's arm. They put their heads together for a final conference.

"This place has got more corridors, passageways, alcoves, and arches than the Waldorf," Barney cautioned. "Let the floor plan slip out of your mind for a second and your bearings fog up."

Jim nodded. "I'm sure Aqaban put Mr. High Mucky-Muck in the fancy suite on the second floor. The ruling caliph of the time built it for the biggest cheeses among the VIP's who came calling."

"We're cutting it fine," Barney remarked.

"Don't we always? But we pick up the pieces."

Their eyes met in the faint light. Each felt the tension in the other.

"Good luck," Barney said.

Their hands met in a brief, warm clasp. Then Barney moved away and disappeared with hardly a rustle of a leaf.

Jim waited five minutes before he stepped from the screening shrubbery. The palace loomed over him, its mass dwarfing a human figure. The windows along this side were mostly dark, the small balconies jutting shadows.

Casually, Jim strolled along a walkway to the rear courtyard. As if he were a guest taking an appreciative, after-dinner amble about the grounds, he paused to look at the varicolored lights of a fountain. From the corner of his eye he studied the wing of the palace, fitting the nearest exit against the mental floor plan he unrolled in his mind.

He turned and moved quietly to a lighted arch. Ahead lay a silent, empty corridor. About thirty feet away a spiral stairway with a wrought-iron railing rose to the second floor.

With quicker steps, he closed the distance. Then, as his hand touched the wrought-iron railing, his knuckles went white. A young servant girl in flowing skirt, drawstring blouse, and sandals was padding down the stairway.

She saw Jim and pressed to one side. Smiling, he mounted the steps. He paused in passing her.

"Quite some excitement in the palace this evening," he remarked.

"Yes, sir." Her eyes were demurely cast down.

"Postponed an appointment with His Excellency. But what member of a trade mission," he continued with a laugh, "could complain of delay in such surroundings?"

"Is there anything you wish, sir?"

"Oh, no. Just had a stroll about the gardens."

She stole a glance at him. "The palace is so big. Have I seen you before, sir?"

"I don't think so." Jim smiled. "I would remember a girl so attractive. I'm associated with Comrade Zovoloff's efforts."

"Yes, sir. If you will excuse me, sir."

With a pleasant nod, Jim continued up. At the head of the stairs, he glanced back. The maid wasn't looking back. She reached the corridor and turned. There was nothing suspicious in her movements. A held breath slipped through Jim's lips.

He was within a few yards of the VIP suite. He moved along the corridor with cat-quick feet, then stopped at the tall, hand-carved door.

With a quick look up and down the hallway, he put his ear close to the door panel. The room was quiet.

Then Jim heard a man clear his throat and the rumble of a pushed-back chair.

Jim lifted his hand and knocked softly.

"Just a minute!" The door was a barrier that didn't entirely soften Zovoloff's voice. In all probability, Jim thought, Zovoloff was preparing a message to be radioed to his bosses and needed a minute to stash his code book.

Jim heard the carpet-muffled thud of footsteps. Zovoloff opened the door. The sight of Phelps was totally unexpected. For a second or two, Zovoloff was speechless.

"The corridor is a bit drafty," Jim suggested.

With obvious uncertainty, Zovoloff edged aside. Jim stepped into the room, and Zovoloff closed the door.

Zovoloff held onto the handle, trying to pull himself together before he turned. Then he looked Jim up and down. "Well, Mr. Phelps, you do have a knack for appearing in the most curious places."

"A habit that's sometimes profitable." Jim scanned the sumptuous sitting room, the plush furnishings, the wall murals, the French doors, and the elevated terrace beyond.

"I take it that you're not merely appreciating my quarters," Zovoloff said.

"Now that you mention it, no. Although they're quite elegant."

"The elegance covers up the bugging devices. They're here. I located them easily. I haven't had a conversation I wanted to keep confidential in this room—as yet."

"I nominate this one," Jim said.

"If I yield to curiosity and listen to you, the bugging devices are momentarily inactive." Zovoloff saw the question in Jim's eyes and added, "His Excellency right now has pressing need elsewhere for the guard who usually sits in the adjoining room under a headset. Street fighting has broken out in some parts of the city—fools with rocks and a few old contraband guns against Aqaban's half-tracks. His heavy-handed search for the young Negro is touching off some of the more desperate people."

"I'm glad we can talk freely," Jim said. "I'm finding Aqaban's methods a bit irritating myself."

"Really?" Zovoloff crossed to a table where attractive snack dishes had been set out. He chose a cracker smeared with caviar as if he had nothing better to do. "In what way has His Excellency fallen short of your expectations?"

"I expect you could answer that."

"I didn't come here expecting to do business with a knight in shining armor, Mr. Phelps."

"Neither did I. But there are limits."

Zovoloff nibbled the hors d'oeuvre. "Too bad, Mr. Phelps. But you're wasting your time. You and I have nothing in common. We can be of no advantage to each other."

"I wouldn't be too sure."

"I am very sure." Zovoloff punctuated his words with a stabbing finger. "By coming here, you have told me one thing. You are out in the cold, and you know it. The members of your cartel might as well try to sit on their bank vaults and hatch their millions!"

Jim sidled to a chair, gripped the arms, and lowered himself slowly. His face was pale, as if with an effort to control a mounting, inner fury. "What else did Aqaban spill about me?"

Zovoloff guffawed. "Aqaban? Don't add that to his list of sins."

"Then you made a very good guess about me."

"Not at all," Zovoloff said. "I know all about you, Phelps."

"*All* about me?" Jim let his eyes widen to the incredible. "I wouldn't be too sure about that, Captain."

"I grew more certain with each tick of the clock," Zovoloff crowed. "The international combine got wind of Dr. Belorra's researches. When he was detained here, they reasoned, easily enough, that the good scientist had come up with results that Aqaban wanted to keep for himself. You were chosen to contact Miriam Belorra in Rome, explore the possibilities, and slip into Masacar if the outlook was good."

Zovoloff sucked a final bit of caviar from a fingertip. His lips curled a cold smile. "But you have failed, Phelps. And I think you'll find it much harder to get out of Masacar than it was to get in."

"I've been down before," Jim told him, "but I never did like the feel of the canvas against my back."

"This time you're out for good. The reaction of the people to Aqaban's searching guardsmen is a development I hadn't exactly expected, but one that gives me considerable pleasure. When the sparks of rebellion begin to fly, who can predict the size of the fire? Aqaban will get the message, even if he is able to put down the isolated flareups without much trouble. He will be hungrier than ever for our tanks, guns, planes. He'll stop his double-dealing—and I'll fly out of Masacar with what I came after."

Jim pushed out of the chair. "How did you learn about me?"

"Miriam Belorra is here in the palace," Zovoloff said, "and it gives me pleasure to tell you."

"Miriam?" Jim echoed. He shook his head. "You're barking up the wrong tree, Captain. I won't believe that Miss Belorra sold out and dropped me to the wolves."

"She isn't a guest." Zovoloff's tone rubbed it in. "She's in that rather dreary section—in the cell with her father."

Jim stared. Then something inside of him began to change in swift degrees. A new light stole into his eyes. A bubble of laughter formed inside of him. It gathered force and broke the bonds of silence. His body shook with it. The sound of it filled the room. Jim's eyes moistened from it.

Zovoloff was beside him in three quick steps. His heavy-knuckled hand seized Jim's shoulder.

"What's the matter with you, Phelps? What's so very, very funny?"

Jim spluttered with the effort to stop laughing. "You," he gasped, one more laugh popping out. "You were so cocksure. You had me convinced for a moment that you really knew it all."

"You'd better explain yourself, Phelps!"

"Aqaban, you—even me." Jim flipped out a handkerchief to dab the laughter tears from the corners of his eyes. "All of us outwitted by a harmless but tough-minded scientist."

"If you're implying what I think you are. . . ."

Jim shoved Zovoloff's hand from his shoulder with a challenging gesture. "I'm not implying, I'm telling you straight out. There were three—not two—residents in the Belorra household, besides the servants, that night. The night Aqaban's dirty hand reached for Dr. Hasman Belorra. Three left the house—two men, friends of about the same age, and Miriam Belorra. The three later separated, to confuse Aqaban's human bloodhounds."

Zovoloff stepped back for the full, penetrating view of Jim's face.

"One man was taken at the oasis and brought back," Jim said. "Knowing nothing about a second man, the guards assumed their captive was Dr. Belorra. They beat his protests back into his lips in those moments when they might have learned the truth. Why should they question? The hunt had ended in a jubilant success. The details all dovetailed, even to the fugitive's general description. But how many millions of men around the Mediterranean basin fit the same description? Look at the hundreds of faces and builds, all alike, on any Semitic street."

"I won't believe it!"

"You mean," Jim insisted, "you don't want to believe it. But think about it. The captive figured he was done for, in any event. If he told the truth, he faced torture, Aqaban's vicious attempts to find out where the real Dr. Belorra had gone. The captive grabbed the last chance to buy time for himself, to defy Aqaban, and to give a dear friend and valued scientist time to get away."

A dampish gleam was barely beginning to show on Zovoloff's high forehead.

"By the time the guards dragged the captive in and threw him at Aqaban's feet," Jim said, his voice soft, subtly persuasive in its apparent candor, "the misidentity of the captive had been pretty well established. Word had been flashed ahead. Aqaban, between kicking up his heels in joy, had pats on the back for the guards."

Zovoloff jerked his gaze from Jim's like an unwilling subject fighting hypnosis. "A scientist also . . ." he muttered to himself.

"Naturally," Jim said. "He and Belorra. You know the old saw. Birds of a feather. We all pick our friends from our own flock."

Zovoloff curled a brow. "How about the truth drugs Aqaban used?"

"Pete's sake!" Jim exploded. "You expect everything from me—the contemptible enemy of a few short minutes ago? Do some of your own homework, big cat. With their knowledge, maybe Dr. Belorra and his friend prepared each other for the eventualities of capture before they split. They were desperate—but they were also brilliant, tough, realistic. Probabilities wouldn't escape their notice, certainly!"

"A moment ago you said the guards gave the captive no chance to protest when they ran him down at the oasis."

"I'm sure they didn't." Jim nodded. "Maybe he tried to protest, maybe he didn't. Who knows? I'm sure he didn't willingly get caught. But I'm also sure he tried to throw the guards off the real Dr. Belorra's trail. Dr. Belorra's discovery was far more important to the world than both men put together. Both would have seen their duty to put the preservation of the Belorra formula above everything else."

A baleful smoldering clouded Zovoloff's eyes. "Miriam Belorra came back," he pointed out.

"Because she also believed the captive was her father," Jim said. "But the moment she saw him she knew. It was the first thing she told me when she returned to the hotel. She said she was so stunned she almost betrayed herself. She was afraid Aqaban had noticed the false note in the reunion."

Zovoloff's teeth clicked. "So that was what was on the upstart's mind after her visit."

"You're clever," Jim said. "You'd never buy a pig in a poke. You'd question every claim advanced by anyone trying to bargain with you. You wouldn't miss a detail or the smallest chance to hammer a deal into the shape you wanted. I seriously thought that by this time you would have dug into the truth. Neither of us needs Aqaban. That popinjay really thought he had Belorra. Since he hasn't, maybe we could deal with *your* team, not Aqaban."

Zovoloff's nostrils flared. "Do you know where Belorra is?"

Jim shrugged. "He probably fell in with one of the small, wandering desert tribes. I'd guess he's living with them until he has the opportunity to get out. But I'm sure we can find him, if you give us a little help. You keep friend Aqaban off our necks. We'll turn up Belorra."

"And simply hand him over?"

"Of course not! We thought we could make a relatively simple deal with Aqaban. We can't. So we'll bill you for about our first ten years' profits. We salvage what we can. We're happy, and we put our loose millions to work someplace else. You get what you're after. You're happy. Aqaban will still have your military toe in his door, and that should make even him happy."

Zovoloff mused his way to the table and looked idly at the food dainties. "What would keep us from searching out the real Dr. Belorra ourselves?" he asked.

"Oh, come now." Jim's hand flicked, disparaging the thought. "You send in a flock of agents searching for Belorra, and you know what would happen instantly. The big powers on the other side wouldn't like the smell of the wind at all. You'd get your fingers pretty sticky. But us, we can pop Belorra like a pea from a pod. And you can continue to sit at the United Nations and blame the other side for the hanky-panky in Masacar."

Zovoloff massaged his chin. "You're very good with words, Phelps."

"I'm even better with action," Jim said. "Come along and I'll prove to you that the man in the cell isn't Hasman Belorra." His eyes glittered as if with greed and cunning. "Between Miriam Belorra and the captive, we might even get an immediate lead on what the real Belorra said and did, a clue to Belorra's flight plan."

Jim saw temptation overpower everything else in Zovoloff's eyes.

14. "JUST GRAB AND HANG ON!"

A BLENDING of luxury hotel and military fortress, the palace was a gilded hive where activity never ceased. The rhythm usually followed a predictable pattern, peaking during the day when His Excellency dictated the nation's affairs, relaxing in the after-dinner hours, sinking to low ebb after midnight when charwomen polished floor tiles and guards yawned at their posts.

Tonight the cycle had shifted. The dinner hour preceded no letup. The rising sense of tension made the day seem dull by comparison. Whispered rumors flew with mercurial speed in the servants' quarters and through the depleted ranks of guardsmen: The young black man was descended from the last, late caliph,

197

claiming rights to a throne that no longer existed. Foreign powers were using him as a tool. Parachutists had landed. A tank column had rumbled across the western frontier. Agents of the pretender-prince were setting fires in downtown Masarium.

Everybody had answers—except His Excellency. He was in the radio communications and command post located in a battlement on the northeast corner of the palace, where once archers had continued to fight when the outer wall had been breached.

Aqaban shivered with rage as he listened to the reports from staff cars. Thrusting through the tinny shortwave static, the words of officers deployed across the city added up to an unexpected and sinister meaning: The louts had turned up a hornet's nest, but not the young Negro.

A hammering, ropelike vein across Aqaban's forehead was a clue to the headache that threatened to shatter his skull.

What had happened? In truth, how had it all come about? At the outset, everything had seemed so beautifully arranged. Trade the Belorra formula for a guarantee of power. Enjoy a magnificent victory dinner. Send Captain Stefan Zovoloff home.

Then the joyful certainties had shriveled by degrees. It was as if, Aqaban thought, he were reaching for a tidbit and invisible fingers kept inching the plate just out of his grasp.

His savage glower vented the faintest part of his feelings on the radio operator. "Advise me of developments. I'm going to the dungeon. A man and young woman are overdue for some straight answers!"

"Yes, Excellency," the man under the headset acknowledged meekly.

Aqaban strode across the room, his thin breathing sizzling his lips.

At the same moment Aqaban touched the doorknob, there was important activity in other parts of the palace.

A young Negro in pantaloons and jerkin dawdled from the servants' quarter with a mop and bucket in his hands.

A guard at the doorway to the dungeon snapped to attention as two men approached. He recognized one of them, Captain Stefan Zovoloff.

"Open up," Zovoloff said.

"Sir?" the guard trailed off the word hesitantly.

"Don't you know who I am?" Zovoloff demanded.

"Yes, sir."

Zovoloff thrust his hard-chinned face and bristling, military brush of brown hair within inches of the guard's eyes. "Then you know better than to question my order."

"But His Excellency. . . ."

"I'll take full responsibility," Zovoloff said. "Or would you rather lose those corporal's stripes and spend sixty days in the guardhouse?"

The guard drew the bolt, pulled back the door, and clicked his heels.

Phelps followed Zovoloff down the worn, stone stairway to the partially underground corridor below. The hollow echo of their footsteps broke a silence that seemed as old as the palace itself.

Zovoloff stopped at the door of the Belorra cell, gripped the iron bolt, and grunted as he worked it back in its slot.

Responding to Zovoloff's strength, the corrosion-scaled iron portal yielded with a reluctant outcry from rusty hinges.

Cinnamon Carter stood stiffly in the middle of the cell, her anxious eyes on the opening door. Behind her, Rollin Hand lay on his side on the lumpy cot. His body was curled slightly, facing toward the slimy wall. Cinnamon's shadow covered his head and shoulders.

Zovoloff studied Cinnamon as he took a slow step into the cell. He glanced past her, at the feet, legs, and waist of the cotton-clad figure on the cot.

"Miss Belorra, I've a few things to ask you and the man there on the cot," Zovoloff said.

"Please, Captain. Everything has been so much for my father. Now that he's getting a little rest, couldn't you. . . ."

"Your father, Miss Belorra? Is he, really?"

Cinnamon frowned. "What do you mean by that, Captain?"

"Perhaps we should let him answer," Zovoloff said.

"Please, Captain!" Cinnamon matched Zovoloff's movement, blocking his way. "Can't you have a little consideration?"

"Stand aside, Miss Belorra!"

Cinnamon threw a beseeching glance at Jim. "Mr. Phelps. . . ."

"Mr. Phelps came to me with an idea," Zovoloff said.

"It's possible we may all be like one big happy family —if you don't try my patience."

Cinnamon's shoulders lifted and dropped in a helpless gesture. She stepped away from the cot. As she did, Rollin Hand rolled over and sat up.

But he was no longer Rollin Hand, at least in appearance. Neither did he look like Dr. Belorra.

Zovoloff stopped and teetered forward on his toes. His jaw dropped. His eyes jutted slightly as he stared at Rollin. Stared at a face that was, in the first tenth of a second, merely familiar. Then more than familiar. Mirrorlike.

Zovoloff gasped, realizing that he was staring at his own features and bristling brown hair.

"A little rubber mask I prepared in advance, Captain," Rollin said with a smile. "I smuggled it in, taped to my stomach."

Zovoloff's mouth snapped shut. His shocked muscles jerked life into themselves. "Phelps, what's the meaning of this?"

Jim had pulled what appeared to be a plastic-cased ball-point pen from his jacket pocket. It wouldn't have drawn a second look from a searcher or interrogator. But Zovoloff seemed suddenly to know that the pen, like so many things connected with this man Phelps, wasn't what it seemed to be.

Seeing the tip of the pen pointed at him, Zovoloff threw himself to one side. The pen clicked. A tiny dart was suddenly dangling from Zovoloff's right cheek. Eyes wild and bewildered, he knocked the dart away with a slashing of his hand. The gesture was as useless as a blow at a bee after it has already stung.

Zovoloff bunched at Jim in a quick movement. Rollin's weight descended on the captain from behind. He clamped a hand over Zovoloff's mouth for the few seconds required for the drug to take effect.

Jim sprang forward to help Rollin. They eased Zovoloff onto the cot.

"Sure you heard enough of his voice for a reasonably good imitation?" Phelps asked, his quick fingers unbuttoning Zovoloff's jacket.

Rollin unbuckled the captain's belt and then moved to his feet to tug at the trousers cuffs. "No, Phelps," Rollin said. "I didn't hear enough to give a reasonably good imitation—but a perfect one!"

Jim had to murmur in admiration. Perfect was the word. Rollin's mimicry was unbelievable. Jim, despite his knowing better, was almost certain that Zovoloff himself had uttered the words.

Jim rolled the captain out of his shirt and threw a blanket over the form.

Rollin pulled on Zovoloff's clothing. Knotting the necktie, he commanded, "Miss Belorra, you will face me when I speak to you about your father!"

Cinnamon stepped back into the cell. "Yes, sir, Captain Stefan Zovoloff."

"No premature celebrations," Jim warned. "Masacar looks like a mighty big country when you're stuck in the middle of it!"

Outside the main doorway to the dungeon, the guard frowned as a young man ambled forward carrying a bucket with a mop sticking out of it.

"What are you doing in this area?" the guard asked suspiciously.

"What does it look like?" Barney Collier parked the bucket and mop against the wall. He stretched, yawned, and scratched his chest. "Been a long day, and I still got to clean a cell for them to put the Belorra girl in."

The guard, a short, bull-shouldered man, grumbled, "Well, all right. But snap it up."

"Snap it up, snap it up," Barney muttered. "That's all you hear around this place."

The guard was putting some weight against the door. It inched open with a rasping of steel.

The guard turned and started to move aside for Barney to pass. Instead, he hesitated. His frown deepened as he watched Barney pick up the bucket.

"Wait a minute!" The guard was suddenly a barrier in the open doorway. "I've never seen you before. You're new around here."

"Slightly," Barney said.

"Young . . . Negro . . ." the guard murmured, half under his breath. He raised the sound level a notch. "His Excellency is taking the city apart looking for a fellow who answers your description."

"How about that?"

"I think I'd better check on you. If you're who you say you are, you won't mind."

"If I was who I haven't at all said I was"—Barney set down the bucket and propped the mop against the wall—"I wouldn't mind one bit."

He raised up and lifted a friendly smile to the

guard's face. He extended his right arm. A hissing sound and a faint ribbon of vapor shot from his curled fingers. That single squeeze of nerve gas from the small vial was sufficient. The guard had time only for a bewildered expression before his knees turned to water.

The guard folded in slow motion. Barney ducked and grabbed the man's limp arm, letting the weight collapse across his shoulders.

Muscles straining and legs wobbling under the guard's bulk, Barney carried the man down the stone steps. The first cell on his right was empty, the door open.

Barney struggled in, slowly bent forward, and let the guard peel away from him onto a bare cot made of rough boards.

His movements quickening, Barney stepped out and closed the cell door. He ran up the steps, grasped the edge of the main door, started it swinging, and jerked his fingers out of the way as the door met its thick metal casing.

He raced down the stairs and through the corridor to the Belorra cell, where he drew up short. Three people turned to look at him, Phelps and the images of Miriam Belorra and Zovoloff. A fourth figure was an indistinct form on the cot, covered from head to toe by a dirty blanket.

"My young black friend," the voice of Zovoloff roared, "hasn't His Excellency taken you in tow yet?"

Barney grinned. "Beautiful, Rollin, both the voice and the mask you worked up from the photographs.

For a second you had even me wondering who was which."

Phelps was reaching up, stripping the iron-colored tape and lifting the bars from the high, narrow window.

"Okay," he said. "Out we go. Ladies first, Cinnamon. I'll give you a boost. We've a jeep parked and waiting in the archaeological diggings. Passengers, however, will not qualify for life insurance!"

His Most Exalted Excellency, Janar Aqaban, the iron hand of Masacar, ground his teeth as he drew up at the dungeon entrance. Another of those irritating inexplicables. The squad for duty here was hand-picked. Each knew it was worth his hide to abandon his post for one moment during a tour of duty. Yet at this moment the main doorway was guarded by nothing more than empty air.

"I'll make him wish. . . ." Aqaban's hoarse threat broke off as he noticed the position of the bolt. He grabbed the door and tugged it open.

"Guard?" he inquired from the top of the stairway. The overhead lights in their steel-mesh cages seemed strangely bright. The silence was a menacing tug.

Aqaban licked his lips, drew in a breath, and scurried down the worn steps. He slammed to a halt at the doorway of the Belorra cell. His hands grabbed the door frame.

His eyes squeezed shut, as if by some miracle this action could repopulate the empty cell with Belorra and his daughter.

He heard the snapping of a dry twig outside.

He paid no attention to the shadowy, lumpy blanket on the cot as he threw himself at the window. Grabbing the ledge, he pulled his chin up to the level of the empty oblong.

Out there on the grounds he saw movement. The flicker of a girlish form disappearing in the tropical garden, two men hurrying close behind her.

"Stop!" Aqaban shouted.

The two men threw looks over their shoulders just before they dived into the covering foliage.

"Zovoloff! Phelps!" Aqaban yelled. "Come back. You traitors . . . you. . . ."

He needed the breath for more important commands. He quickly wriggled himself shoulders first through the window, rolling on the soft grass outside.

He bounced to his feet. "Guards!" He cupped his hands about his mouth. "Guards! Pigs, where are you? This is your leader. *Guards!*"

Pounding footsteps preceded the appearance of two brutish-looking men in fawn-colored uniforms. Aqaban grabbed the first arrival by the arm. "They've broken out. I couldn't see clearly, but I'm sure Phelps and Zovoloff were with them. They're hiding in the shrubbery there. Drag them out!"

Beating his fists together, Aqaban paced impatiently, not taking his eyes from the shadows where the guards were thrashing.

"Excellency. . . ." A guard's voice was a floating hesitation. "No one is here."

"They must be! They couldn't have gotten out

without my seeing them! I've stayed right here to watch!"

"But Excellency...."

"Look harder, you donkeys!" Aqaban stamped his feet.

A yelp of pain came from the screening shrubbery. "Excellency ... a place in the sod ... my foot broke through ... Excellency, they have a tunnel."

Aqaban scrubbed clammy sweat from his forehead with the back of his hand. His mind was a fiery whirlpool. Phelps and Zovoloff ... the Belorra formula.... His teeth ground. A sense of outrage almost blinded him for a moment. Did they actually think they could do this to him and get away with it?

"Quickly!" he shouted. "I want a half-track armed with a machine gun!" Fists clenched, he screamed at the guard who crashed from the shrubbery. "At once! Before I'm through they'll be writing confessions—all over the mildewed dungeon walls!"

Everybody was too occupied with efforts to remain inside the careening, bouncing, bucking jeep to say anything about Jim Phelps's driving. If anything, they would have urged him to greater speed as the narrow rutted streets rushed at the headlights.

Rollin was in the seat beside Jim, Cinnamon and Barney in back. Jim gave the steering wheel a twist, and the jeep slewed, then kicked its rear end straight. The long sweep of the airport was before them.

The jeep quickly ate the distance toward the administration building. The airport lay dark and silent, the night breeze off the desert sowing a film of dust from the empty parking area at the ad building.

Jim's eyes strained as he looked at the silvery gleam of the airplane poised on the hangar tarmac.

"Rollin," Jim said.

Holding the edge of the windshield with one hand, the back of the seat with the other, Rollin Hand refused to look at Jim.

"Captain Zovoloff." Jim tried again.

Rollin turned his head. "Yes, Phelps?"

Jim opened his mouth, then closed it. A tight grin tugged his lips. "Nothing," he said, braking near the hangars. "You're carrying the ball."

The jeep dipped its nose in a stop a dozen yards from the plane waiting so patiently for Zovoloff.

Rollin leaped out and strode toward the plane. "Comrades," he yelled, and it was Zovoloff's voice, "I need your help—out here. Something of tremendous importance has come up!"

A dim figure showed its outlines in the open door of the jet's cabin. The pilot turned on a powerful hand flashlight. The beam bathed the figure standing beside the plane.

"Well, move. Both of you!" Rollin snapped his fingers. Behind him, the others were getting out of the jeep. In the far distance, the headlights of an armored half-track were sudden fireflies in the night. "We don't have to toady to that fool Aqaban any longer," Rollin explained quickly. "We have the formula! These are the people who helped. They have spared our country the miserable burden of Masacar. Hurry now and get the things from the jeep. Then home, Comrades—to our hero medals!"

The pilot and copilot saw the face of Zovoloff and heard the happy instructions delivered in Zovoloff's voice. Men trained to obey, they tumbled from the plane and rushed quickly to Rollin to shake the hand they thought belonged to Zovoloff.

Barney, an unobtrusive shadow, quietly lifted his hand and gave the vial of nerve gas two quick squeezes.

The pilot and copilot were so close to Jim and Rollin that the two IMF agents caught the crumpling men almost effortlessly.

Jim and Rollin lowered the men to the tarmac.

"Jim," Barney said in a talking-about-the-weather tone, "I see some headlights pell-melling it on the airport road. Could be we've got company?"

Jim sprang up from beside the limp pilot and copilot. "Into the plane, all of you!"

"Jim," Cinnamon started to protest.

"I know," Jim said. "Three still unaccounted for. Willy, Dr. Belorra, and Miriam. But we'll need every second when they show. So how about you getting your pretty self into that aircraft!"

Jim watched the distant headlights. Feverish sweat burned his face. It had been Willy's job to lead Dr. Belorra and Miriam from the ruined Belorra house to the airport and stay in hiding until the rest of the team showed up. But so many of Aqaban's men were patrolling the city, stopping people, asking questions. . . .

"Willy, Willy," Jim whispered, "the finest sight on earth right now would be your beautifully homely face."

He stopped breathing as the headlights of an armored half-track arced across the farthest edge of the airport.

Then the sound of running feet jerked Phelps about. Three figures closed on him from the dark corner of the ad building.

Sweaty, grimy, Willy, Dr. Belorra, and Miriam heard Jim's urgent command: "Quick! The others are already in the plane."

"Had to do some dodging," Willy gasped. "Patrols all over town. . . ."

Willy reached the side of the plane. He grasped Dr. Belorra's arm and boosted him to the cabin door. He lifted Miriam, then climbed in himself, reaching back to grab Jim's hand and yank him bodily into the aircraft.

Jim bolted for the pilot's cabin while Willy slammed the door.

"Safety belts, everybody," Jim said in passing. "And if there aren't enough seats in this little job, just grab and hang on!"

Rollin was already in the copilot's seat, the Zovoloff mask ripped off.

Jim threw himself into the pilot's seat. The markings on the instruments were in a foreign language, but Rollin could read it, and Jim had no qualms about getting the feel of the controls.

Through the window he could see the half-track

coming. The brilliant white uniform marked a man standing in it, screaming orders.

"Ready with one," Rollin said.

"Start one."

The machine gun was a winking eye. Jim and Rollin ducked as a tracer punched through the cabin window and screamed through the roof.

Number one engine whined.

"Ready with two," Rollin said.

"Start two."

Number two engine snarled.

Jim hit the controls hard. He heard a brief rattle as machine-gun bullets struck metal. Then the runway stretched long before Jim.

"How about some juice, old friend?"

"Why not?" Rollin replied. "Let's see how fast this baby will go. Must admit Zovoloff's boys kept her at the ready."

As the jet lifted off and screamed like a lance toward the heavens, Jim had one final glimpse of the scene on the ground. The half-track stood forlorn and ineffectual, the white-uniformed man seeming to wilt to nothing.

A half hour later, with the Mediterranean sparkling with moonlight far below, Jim returned to his pilot's seat from an inspection of the main cabin. He mused on a star in the sky, aware that Rollin was watching him from the copilot's side.

"Everybody fine," Jim remarked. "No sweat." He thought for a moment. "I wouldn't give a plugged ruble for Aqaban's future."

"Or Zovoloff's," Rollin added. "You fly her awhile, pal. I feel like relaxing."

Jim took hold of the controls. The sky was clear and a million miles wide. Jim set a course for Rome and the American embassy.

From the main cabin came the sound of singing: "Sailing ... sailing ... over the bounding main. ..."

Whitman ADVENTURE and MYSTERY Books

SPORTS STORIES
Throw the Long Bomb
Hot Rod Road

BRAINS BENTON
The Missing Message
The Counterfeit Coin
The Stolen Dummy
The Roving Rolls
The Waltzing Mouse
The Painted Dragon

DONNA PARKER
At Cherrydale
Special Agent
On Her Own

WALT DISNEY PRESENTS
Peter Pan
The Gnome-Mobile
The Swiss Family
   Robinson

Whitman
REG. U.S. PAT. OFF.

TELEVISION FAVORITES
The Mod Squad

Land of the Giants

Ironside

Mission: Impossible

Star Trek

Hawaii Five-O

The High Chaparral

The Rat Patrol

Garrison's Gorillas

The Monkees

Bonanza

Lassie·
   Bristlecone Pine
   Smelters' Cave

The Invaders

Gunsmoke